WATERMAN

WATERMAN

A SANDY TALE

لاالدلو"بج

AD-DALW

OSKAR FREYSINGER

Translated by Rudolph Bader

Illustrations by Alexandru Trifu

RESOURCE *Publications* · Eugene, Oregon

WATERMAN
A Sandy Tale

Resource Publications
An Imprint of Wipf and Stock Publishers
199 W. 8th Ave., Suite 3
Eugene, OR 97401

www.wipfandstock.com

PAPERBACK ISBN: 978-1-6667-3178-1
HARDCOVER ISBN: 978-1-6667-2468-4
EBOOK ISBN: 978-1-6667-2469-1

JANUARY 7, 2022 9:58 AM

Contents

First Day

THE HEAVY AIR OVER the desolate plain shimmered in the boiling heat. I could twist and turn as much as I liked; in all four directions there was nothing but the slumbering sky and the desert. Suddenly, there appeared that hazy spot on the horizon. At first, I took it for a dusty speck on my eyeglasses. However, since the speck wasn't moving with the movements of my head it had to be something else. As it was growing in size I assumed it might be a *fata morgana* due to the reflections of the hot air. But this assumption, also, had to be abandoned, for the speck, gradually changing into a hazy shadow that was branching out, didn't recede but was moving closer. Half an hour later, a tree peeled itself from the dreariness and seemed to reach for the sky with its desperate twigs. Coming closer yet, I recognized a second shape, which soon revealed itself as a cowering human form.

When, soon after, I brought my four-wheel-drive to a stop in front of this strange double shape, I found an acacia sheltering a nomad clad in an indigo-blue *gandura*, the long gown of the Tuareg. There was no camel in sight, no other human presence, only this cowering man and the tree overhanging him, and the glimmering furnace of the Sahara. How had this man come to this spot? Had his camel bolted or died? Was he waiting for some redeeming intervention? That didn't appear to be the case since he hadn't budged when I approached. No jumping up, no desperate gesticulation with his arms, no cries for help, nothing, even though the engine noise must have been clearly audible from far away in this brooding silence. Was the man asleep? Was he too exhausted to get up? On the ground next to him there was a *guerba* three quarters filled with water. I alighted and approached the half-veiled figure. Two dark eyes were peering at me, surrounded by deep wrinkles. The man appeared to be quite old, an impression which couldn't be fully ascertained because of the *tagelmust*—the facial veil of the Tuareg—and his sun-parched skin. Despite the numerous layers of cloth under his broad *gandura* I concluded that his body had to be extremely lank and gaunt. I stepped up to him.

"*Assalamu alaykum*," Peace to you.

"*Assalam*," Peace.

His voice was calm but firm. There wasn't a trace of exhaustion or even desperation. The old man was squatting under his tree in the middle of nowhere as if this was the most natural thing in the world.

I cleared my throat and—not being familiar with the Berber language—I asked him in French if I could be of any assistance to him, if he might want a lift. He shook his head.

"*Tout va très bien*," Everything is fine.

This reply was to be expected. He really didn't look like a hitchhiker to me.

Suddenly he seemed to remember something and asked me if I had a gas cooker with me.

I said yes, walked back to my Land Rover, dug out the desired appliance from the load compartment and returned to him.

Nodding his head with thanks, he accepted the cooker, before retrieving from his clothes a small round metal pot with a cranked spout, two tiny glass cups, a sugar bag and some green tea leaves, and he began to prepare tea. When he had completed the task and the gas cooker began to sing away he made an inviting gesture.

Obediently, I sat down.

It was *l'eyerewal*, the time of the vertical shadows, when nothing in the desert moves. If the acacia roof had not given us shelter, we would have been mummified presently, my own body long before his, because it was sweating more heavily than his heat-proof nomad's body.

Soon, the water came to the boil, and he poured the frothy tea into the two cups, while deftly swaying the pot up and down.

"*Alhamdulillah*,"—thanks be to Allah—he said and sipped at his cup.

The tea was delicious, bitter as life, as is fitting for the first round.

When I judged we had exchanged enough polite phrases I asked him what he was doing in this godforsaken spot without his camel.

"A godforsaken place?" His veil having been shifted slightly downwards, I could detect his forbearing smile. "There is no god-forsaken place wherever there is a human being."

"By god-forsaken I meant remote."

He corrected me again.

"Wherever there is a human presence, there is the center of the world. Especially if there are two people sitting together having tea, as we are."

Now I had to smile, too. In a way, he was right.

"There are as many centers of the world as there are human beings," he continued in a cautionary tone. "Wherever there is consciousness, the universe turns around it."

I objected by suggesting that from an economic and social point of view, places like New York or Paris could more likely be considered centers of the world, rather than a lonely acacia in the *Ténéré*, the desert of deserts, one of the hottest places on earth, which was rightfully called "Land of Emptiness" in the language of the nomads.

He took his time for his answer and seemed to balance the pros and cons of the matter.

Then he put the last touch to his argumentation:

"Possibly. But in such a big city it is very difficult to feel at the center of the world. One gets lost in diversity."

After a brief pause, he added: "You can only be the center of the world in complete solitude. You need the void in order to relate to yourself and to become one with the universe."

No doubt I had to deal with a remote descendant of Diogenes. If we hadn't been sitting in the shade of an acacia, I might have had the impression I was obscuring his sun rays.

Out of the blue, he asked me what I was about with my noisy vehicle, at a time of the day when nothing ought to be moving.

"I am in charge of a development program for the *Ténéré*."

"You want to develop the void?" he shrewdly asked, confronting me with the absurdity of my undertaking.

"The void is not as empty as it appears to be. We want to revive it. Our aim is to bring back nomadic life to this region." He stared at me as if he hadn't grasped what I had said.

"Bring back nomadic life, you said?"

After repeating my words incredulously, he broke into a loud croaky laughter from which he had difficulty recovering.

I felt rebuked.

Nonetheless, I attempted to explain to him the basic points of our program: the drilling of wells, the development of cattle keeping, the setting up of a market for products from livestock farming, and so on.

Meanwhile, he had regained his composure, and he said in a firm voice which allowed no contradiction: "*C'est absolument fou!* You cannot bring back nomadic life to something that's in perpetual movement. Every single dune is a nomad, every cloud, every grain of sand. The only non-nomadic element on this earth is death."

What was I supposed to reply to this? Every thought seemed to dissolve in my head, even before I could shape it into a coherent argument.

"After all, that is why I am here," the old man said and tripped me again. "I have an appointment with death."

I stared at him unbelievingly. "You have come here to die?"

"Yes," he said casually, as if this was the most natural thing in the world. "I've had a rich and endlessly diverse life. Now my time has run its course. Since I have fulfilled my duties on earth I can quietly step down."

I didn't even manage to pronounce a "but . . . ", his decision hit me as so obvious and natural.

"Strangely Allah seems to have decided to bring me some company before my death," he added mischievously as he was pouring the second cup of tea. "As sweet as love," I thought, as it was appropriate for the second round, according to tradition.

Gradually, the decision grew in me to keep him company, he was such a fascinating individual of the human species. After all, I had as much time as there was sand in the desert.

"If I'm not too much of a disturbance while you're dying, I would like to spend a few hours in your company, to talk to you about God and the world, and to kill time," I daringly said with a pinch of black irony.

"No worries," he said, "you are welcome. Death will hardly be frightened away by our chat under this tree. Nor by the emptiness of the land surrounding us. He is emptiness himself, after all."

Then he gave me his hand.

"My name is Meddur," he said, "As a Targi—singular of Tuareg—born with sand in his eyes, I'm one of those blue nomads who seem to fascinate you strangers so much."

"*Enchanté*," I answered. "Jean Tourel, project leader with the NGO Green Desert, agronomist and geographer."

His facial expression signaled respect.

I stood up and fetched some biscuits from my car, to go with the tea.

"So, you are a *Kel Tamashek*, a Tuareg."

"*Eh oui!* A distant descendant of *Amzir*, son of *Kanaan*, son of *Ham*, and of *Tamazigh*, daughter of *Medjeb*."

I didn't grasp if he meant his great-grandparents or some ancient gods of his cosmogony.

"My camel is my walking garden during the day and my flying carpet during the night, when I ride through the desert, sleeping on its back."

Respect! This Meddur was not only a philosopher but also a gifted poet. If he proved himself to be a prophet, as well, things would be complete, despite the void around us.

"There's one thing you have to know if you want to bring back nomadic life, as you say," he mockingly said. "We were never a nation. We have always been tribes and clans, boundlessly free and independent as those flying water hoses in the sky that you strangers call clouds. In the thousand years of our history, each shifting dune of the desert has taught us that the world means change, that we ourselves are subject to change. Even though the sky above may be as dry as a barren woman's belly, there is a lot of life down here. Particularly at night. Every human being, every atom is a nomad. It's only that many people, especially from your world, seem to have missed that. Or they keep this idea at bay, like the shepherdess the jackal."

I didn't know what to say to this, so I just listened. Enchanted by the magic of the moment and by this man's profound words, and deeply moved by the unexpected mystic experience in this most remote spot on earth, I absorbed what I learned from him like pure, unalloyed water. I cannot repeat everything that the Targi said, but some things instilled themselves indelibly in my mind and have since influenced my life crucially.

Later in the afternoon, he waxed lyrical.

"Listen to the song of the dunes in the breeze, when Allah plays his one-stringed lute *imzad*," he said, "harken to the voices of the stones in the *Aïr* mountains. Among the dark rock walls of the *Ahaggar,* lend your ears to the cries and the lamentations of the people of the void, the *Kel Assuf*—the spirits of the dead—who are so heart rending that the rocks break apart and the stones burst asunder."

In the face of the power of this invocation my critical mind blew out, even before I realized that Meddur was losing himself in his spiritual beliefs, and that the bursting of the rocks was based on the extreme differences in temperature between day and night.

"You are driven by inner winds," the nomad said. "The dunes migrate across your soul. Peace and quiet are illusions. They do not even exist between the storms of the outer world. The desert is a sundial that never stops trickling. It consists of the most flexible particles in the world because they are unbound. Only atoms are smaller. And even they are in movement."

Panta rei wrapped up in desert poetry, I thought and objected that the atoms in the sand grains are fixed and inert.

"What difference does this make when the *samum*, the sand-storm, blows the sand in your eyes and ears?" he added. "And there may be things going on in the atoms which we don't know. Every detail is the whole in miniature. For these very reasons the structures of nomadic life have grown like hardwood. Thence also our numerous unwritten laws. Thanks to these, we have been able to achieve and maintain a balance between the world and the humans for over a thousand years."

I could certainly comprehend this. The barrenness of the resources forced the nomads to a symbiosis, to the development of a special type of civilization. Therefore, every one of them shared what scarcity they had. This made for a life-saving balance—provided all of them abided by the rules.

I was overwhelmed. What this nomad was saying, so close to death and quietly sipping his tea, dwarfed everything else I had ever heard before. But the most unbelievable aspect of his case was the complete compatibility of his theory and practice. His actions consistently mirrored his thoughts and vice versa.

The Targi again fumbled with his teapot and, following the unwritten rules of the Sahara, poured tea for the third time.

The tea in the third cup was soothing like the death awaiting him.

So, we sat together for the whole afternoon, sipped tea and waited for the evening.

Our conversations were often interrupted by long silences, until the flow of our words almost dried up. Like the voice of the *imzad*, the one stringed lute of the Tuareg, the absence of words set up a framework that protectively enclosed the quietness of the desert.

First Night

A<small>S NIGHTTIME WAS APPROACHING</small>, I prepared a modest meal with provisions I carried in the Land Rover: rice, some vegetables, and a piece of mutton.

The old man didn't wait to be invited. He dug in as though he wanted to feed himself with sufficient calories for his trip to the next world.

After the blood-red sky had faded on the western horizon, and the celestial carpet embroidered with tiny sparkles had spread across the sky, we admired the constellations above our heads. I pointed out Andromeda, Pegasus, Castor and Pollux. When I drew my fingers around the intricate shape of Cassiopeia he said: "Ah, the back of the camel mare." To Orion he said: "*Amanar*, the caravan leader, and the belt is the camel mare." "In Canopus, he saw a camel stud, and in Aldebaran a herd grazing among the glowing grass of the night.

Amused, I turned to him.

"Your sky is nothing but a camel pasture."

"That's possible, but at least it forms a unity around the camel. Your constellations, on the other hand, lie around like a multitude of carelessly discarded tools. That is no longer a sky but a toolshed in need of repair. Furthermore, the stars don't seem to satisfy you *ikufar*[1]. That's why you constantly attempt to add new ones that move to and fro but never stick to the sky. There is no need for those. The sky is overstocked as it is."

1. infidels

Faced with this striking assessment of the occidental night-sky, I had to smile. On the other hand, I liked the idea of a firmament reflecting the nomads' earthly environment—albeit in an idealized and transfigured form, but still connected with reality—so that the *Kel Tamashek* could read in it the fundamental components of their lives.

"There's one thing you have to know, Jean, if you want to understand the desert," Meddur continued with his explanations. "The camel IS the desert. When you ride on its back you are moved about, up and down, to and fro, as if you were desert sand. Everything is on the move, except the fixed pole rooted in the camel itself that safely takes you to your destination. We humans have been shaped by evolution. Originally, we weren't planned like this, and we only survive by adaptation. The camel, however, is Allah's perfect creation. It shows us our relativity and illustrates the course of life itself. At best, the believer knows but ninety-nine names of Allah. The camel alone knows all the one hundred."

This unusual explanation made me smile. But I could somehow feel the profound truth behind it.

"The camel itself is a sand dune," Meddur continued, "a drifting sand dune, a kind of shifting immovability. It is the hand that Allah offers to humans to guide them through the desert. Just look at the relationship between saddle and humps: they form two semicircles meeting at their apex, one of them open at the top, the other at the bottom, and man is the link between these two infinities. The camel was created even before the world, before the palm trees and the pastures. And shortly after that, the nomad was created in order to become one with it. Together, they constitute the balance between the animal's coldness and human warmth, which is necessary for survival in the desert. The camel is part of its rider, and the rider forms part of the camel. It is only on its back that we nomads can find independence and freedom. Although the camel appears to be slow, it is quite fast. Because it just does what needs to be done. Because it does everything right. Neither too much nor too little. Because it knows the way. And the destination. In contrast, people appear to be fast. But they only rush to hasten their deaths. And death is the slowest thing in the world. For nothing is slower than eternal standstill."

Again, I had to smile at Meddur's ways of presenting certain wisdoms so outlandishly. But he continued immediately, for he seemed to possess inexhaustible knowledge about the camel.

"Without the camel, humans are an alien element in the desert because, unlike the camels they mount, they are incapable of storing water in their tissues. Mounted on the camel, humans merge with the desert and the desert becomes their home. Why do you think the camel always draws the same old bored and condescending face? Because it knows that a person's survival depends on it, whereas it doesn't need a human to survive in the desert.

"Jean, humans are unsteady beings. Not so the camel, because it is made for the desert. Its instinct shows its rider the way. And why? Because the camel comes from the end of the world while humans are only at the beginning. That is why all our newborn babies are baptized with camel urine, our women dip their hair in it, and we call our children guardians of the camels, even before naming them properly."

After a long pause he added:

"The swaying motion of the camel is Allah's breath as it travels through the hot air, praised be Allah, *Alhamdulillah*."

The silence, which opened between us after these words, seemed to be filled with the quiet sound of the heavenly camels' chewing the cud.

Later, I fetched a mat and my down sleeping bag from the car and brought a woolen blanket for the Targi, for it was getting severely cold. If I was about to prolong this nomad's life uninvited, at least he should not be freezing before the cold hand of death would take hold of him. Without comment, he wrapped himself up in my blanket and leaned back against the tree.

I slipped into my sleeping bag and closed my eyes. Behind my eyelids there opened up a heavenly landscape full of glowing camels grazing on sparkling grass stalks.

Later, a soft mumbling noise crawled into my already half absent consciousness, and I vaguely realized that Meddur was reciting his prayers. Then I dropped off into a deep sleep.

Second Day

O N THE FOLLOWING MORNING, at the time of the *ahokkat*—
the little day—the same murmuring woke me up. Yawning,
I peeled myself out of my sleeping bag and stretched my stiff limbs
in the cold morning.

When the Targi had completed his ritual, he sat down under
the tree again and began to prepare his tea.

It was only when the burner began its humming that I realized the complete silence around me. No breeze stirred, no grain
of sand moved, and no pebble rolled by. There was absolutely no
movement apart from the Targi, the growing morning light and
me. Meddur was right: We were the center of the world.

However, I felt sorry for the fact that this only motivated him
to have his tea and wait for death. To insert some life into this
seemingly inexorable intention, I resumed the conversation, asking him about his tribe and his assessment of the survival chances
of the nomads.

Well, he estimated that there wasn't much left to be assessed.
He reached out so far to support his thesis that he appeared to me
like a caravan that, in order to travel from Agadez in the south to
the Bilma Oasis in the north, first rounded the Sahara between the
Atlantic Ocean and the Suez Canal and only then tightened the
loop gradually.

His unstoppable fluency encircled my consciousness like a
sea of dunes around an oasis. It seemed as if he had to shake off
everything that had accumulated in his head and heart during his

long life, before his final silence. But it was fascinating. This fascination remained untainted because, as the center of the world, we were absolutely safe from any disturbance.

He told me about the great historical caravans, the Bilma Caravan transporting salt and dates in autumn, and the Damergu Caravan travelling as far down as Nigeria to exchange the goods from Bilma for cattle, millet, and fabrics. He explained the triangular trade between the Aïr, Bilma and the southern Niger or northern Nigeria, and he described the production and the transport of the *kantu*—the salt stumps mixed with clay—as well as the salt cakes and salt breads, which were made in Bilma. I got the impression that life for the Tuareg moved around a magic triangle of dates, salt, and camels.

He explained that the word "caravan" came from the Persian language and originally meant "protection of trade," which seemed quite evident.

Suddenly his face darkened. His voice began to tremble almost indiscernibly.

"Unfortunately, one day the end of the world came for the Tuareg," he said. "The great drought between 1969 and 1973 gave the final blow to nomadic life north of the Sahel. A man can bear poverty and deprivation just as the camel can bear the scarcity of water, but not the absolute void. We became so weak that most diseases ended in death. Our children died by the thousands, our animals perished from thirst and starvation, despite our efforts. We tried to sell parts of our herds before they starved, but due to the laws of supply and demand the prices plummeted. For a time, we survived with the sale of our women's chains, earrings and bracelets, but our standing crumbled like the camo green on our amulets. In the end we had lost everything. Our lives were hanging on thin threads. There was no other solution than migrating to less dry areas in the south.

"I was hardly an adult when we undertook the big march down into the northern Sahel. We knew we wouldn't come back this time. The trek to the end of the world is a one way trip. At last, as a desolate huddle, we reached Agadez, the Gate to the Desert.

For us, it became the gate to shame because we became *ishumar*[2], *des chômeurs*[3], *oui mon ami, parfaitement, des chômeurs*. We got to know a new *assuf*, the wilderness in the hearts of the people, chaos in a civilized space. In order to survive, we became gatherers roaming the wilderness and struggling from day to day. Due to the scarcity of the wild *ishiben* cereal, we partly began to gather driftwood. But the blemish remained. In the desert we had been kings, in town we were nothing. Especially since the disintegration of our *tawshit*, the laws keeping our tribe together in the wilderness.

"Like the monitor lizard *arata*, we tried to adapt to the colors of our new environment, but these changed too rapidly, being so diverse and vertiginous. At least, I learned French and the strange ways of the townspeople.

"While we, the *Kel Tamashek*, had been migrating from the drought in the north to Agadez, another migration had been taking place to the town from the opposite direction, which I found very puzzling. Why would all those people want to migrate to a more distant north than the north of the Sahara, even beyond the great *Erg* of the *Tikdabra*—the great dune field in northern Algeria—when the *cram cram* grass with its barbs and spikes clung to their clothes and even the migratory birds preferred to travel south? Were they unable to read the signs of nature? Talking to some of those strange nomads, I gathered that they were hoping for a better and happier life in big European cities that were even bigger than Agadez. I shook my head because I already found Agadez quite unbearable. How could anyone be happy in places with ever so many people crowded together in narrow houses, with hustle and bustle and noise all around? Yet, those people seemed to have left a better life down south than we *Kel Tamashek* had left in the heat and drought of the withering desert. They talked of beaches on great lakes they called oceans, of lush rainy seasons, of endless forests and gardens where they could harvest richly several times a year. Those people were probably full of illusions. They were hoping to fulfill a dream and risked ending up as nobodies in

2. Unemployed in Arabic
3. Unemployed in French

19

a no man's land, like we *Kel Tamashek* in Agadez. They let themselves be dazzled by glittering beads in whose glitter they would wither away eventually.

"As I said, their ant trail wound itself north, where they first had to get over the *Ténéré*, then the *Ahaggar*, then the great *Erg*, then at last another expansive sea, and what followed could hardly be easier. It was very cold and inhospitable up there, as I've been told by a man from Agadez who had been in these places. You can't understand people once they have started to migrate without a definite plan. After having stuck like flies to a colorful wall which they felt to be a prison, strangely enough they search for a grey wall elsewhere, only to get stuck again and to dream of colors and freedom. But a wall is a wall. And freedom is a completely different thing.

"We stayed in Agadez for over ten years, and things only got worse. We missed the song of the dunes in the breeze and their constantly changing, sweeping shapes. We missed the silence when the wind dies down, the wide expanse, the darkness around the stars, the true freedom which is conditioned by the irrefutable laws of the desert. We missed the sound of the *imzad* serving the silence. And we missed the strident bickering—the *youyous*—of the women around the campfire. We had become slaves. We had become tainted. We were worth even less than the dubious, decaying mutton that hangs from hooks in the dirty butcher shops in Agadez, vanishing under swarms of flies.

"One day, I heard on the radio that the tree of the *Ténéré* had been run over by a truck. Just imagine: In the middle of a vast area of several hundred thousand kilometers there stands a single obstacle, a tree which, against all the laws of biology, has chosen the hottest spot on earth in order to be safe from humans. Out of respect, no camel nibbles at its leaves, no nomad uses its wood to heat his tea. The tree is taboo. And bang! Here comes a drunken truck driver and actually manages to run it over. The odds are one to billions, but once you have lost your *baraka's* blessing power, even the most impossible thing can hit you.

"The government has since replaced the victim of that regrettable collision with a metal tree—as if one could create life industrially—but dead is dead. The wood from the destroyed acacia came to the national museum. But museums are dead, too. Well, back then in Agadez, we felt like that metal tree, which stands upright and looks like a tree from the distance but is dead inside. And like that museum tree, we no longer stood under *Allah's* blessing.

"I might add that, since that time, not even a sober truck driver has managed to run down the *Ténéré* tree."

The Targi's mouth having become dry from talking, he remembered his tea, completed his preparatory ritual, filled the first bowl, and sipped some of the tart liquid.

I also sipped at the hot bitterness in my cup.

"In the city, music drowns the silence; it isn't at its service," he began again. "It fills up space, it roars in your ears, and it displaces every remnant of peace and quiet. The same goes for the colors, the shapes, the movements, and the smells. Too much is too much! Our sense of perception is getting worn out. The senses lose their acuteness. There is no unity, only contradiction and contrast. There is no depth, only superficiality. In the city, the *fata morgana*, a mirage on the horizon, becomes reality. It materializes. We stumble over it. It limits us. It can be taken prisoner and get sold in the disguise of freedom.

"In the desert, on the other hand, hallucinations remain free, they vanish when we want to grasp them. Mirages in the desert teach us that our gaze must go deeper than the illusion, that it has to go through it in order to find fulfillment, to venture to the oneness which means silence and void. In the desert, our gaze into the distance is a gaze into our innermost. In the city, there is no innermost. Despite the numerous closed rooms there, everything seems turned outwards. How can people find their own selves in such a chaos?

"For this very reason, city people always ask pointless questions like 'where' and 'why'. In the desert, that is not necessary. There, everything is being done that needs to be done and has always been done because it follows out of itself. In the desert, we learn from experience, not from explanations."

Meddur emptied his cup and clicked his tongue.

"*Alhamdulillah,*" he said and then continued.

"After many years of humiliation, we eventually left the city, the place with the closed rooms that are shut off from Allah's eyes. Surrounded by plenty, we had gradually become empty. Now we were hoping for fulfillment from the emptiness of the desert. Meanwhile, I found myself in the middle of my life and was eager to direct my energy towards a challenge that consisted of much more than picking up the leftovers from the table of the city people, like a ringdove.

"All the same, my long stay in the city had not been altogether useless. For it was there that I had learned the signs that matter, in a national program directed at the alphabetization of the nomads. I had followed their endless trail. And I still wonder today through which miracle a few scribblings on a piece of paper can actually produce ever new unexpected worlds in the heads of people. However, even the acquisition of the French language could not tie me to the city in the long run. The call of the true wild was too strong. I yearned for the sandy breath of the *Harmattan,* the crunching of the *Serir,* the pebbly desert under my feet and the rumbling of the *Hammada,* the stony wasteland. I languished for the call of the migratory birds, the dance of the gazelles and the addax, the scurrying of the fennec. My body was eager for the symbiosis with the *mehari,* the riding dromedary, in order to restore the lost balance of my life.

"We moved north with a few camels, goats, and donkeys.

"We went through dry forests and traversed the savanna.

"We crossed several *wadis* and passed rare oases where the sun refreshed its rays in contact with rare palm trees casting some shadows.

"We headed towards the void.

"For the void is our home.

"Once again, we became what we had always remained in our souls, *imohar,* sons of the wind, free and independent human beings. We regained our dignity, our *asshak,* and once again obeyed the decency and integrity, the *tekarakit,* represented by the *imzad.* And we actually found a place which could serve as our starting point for our revival of nomadic life, as certain NGOs call it." At this, he smiled mischievously.

"The more we adapted to the requirements of the desert, the clearer it became to us that the original wilderness is more civilized than the corrupted civilization of the city. We clung to our new situation and recovered our origins. Despite all the conflicts around us, despite the storms, despite death, and despite the warriors of *Boko Haram* and *Al Qaida.*

"Gradually, others joined us: a holy man, whom we call a *marabut,* some blacksmiths and even several serfs. Our clan was growing, and it was welded together, as required by the desert. Years later, I was even elected the clan's chief, its *Amghar,* a dignified position that I held for decades. Now I have reached the end of my life path. As soon as I'm alone again the nightly caravan of the *Kel Assuf* will take me along. *Inshallah.*" The Targi poured a second cup of tea for each of us and sank into a deep rumination. I was lost in my thoughts, too.

Thus, it came that we moved on from our second to our third cup of tea in silence, which seemed somehow logical, since in the face of Death every word is futile. When that third cup was empty, I stood up, knocked the dust from my clothes and stored the mat and the sleeping bag in the Land Rover.

I told Meddur I had to leave. Not seeing me return and without news from me, the people of my organization would be worried, but he could keep the blanket and the gas cooker.

He moved his head left and right and looked up at the sky doubtfully.

"A start so short before noon is not a good idea," he commented and sank back into his brooding silence.

He might have been right if I'd been traveling with a traditional caravan, but in a fairly new Land Rover full of electronics and all the latest gadgets there was no need to worry about the time of the day. It just drives, as it is expected to do.

So, I waved away his objection, shook hands with him in farewell and got behind the wheel.

Ten minutes later, I was still sitting behind the wheel, and I hadn't moved an inch. The Land Rover couldn't be convinced to start. It just roared like a metal camel when I turned the ignition key.

Merde! Shit! I was stuck. What now? Since, of all places, I was trapped in the center of the world, I couldn't get a signal on my mobile phone and so I couldn't call anyone for help either.

"With a camel, this wouldn't happen," said the Targi smiling. "But camels are not so stupid as to walk through the *Ténéré* at the time of the vertical shadows."

His comment made me angry. The time of the day had nothing to do with the car's ignition. He was perfectly aware of that.

What now? I panicked, bordering on desperation. The fact that the Targi wanted to die here within the next few hours was his problem, but as for myself, I had other plans than a trip to the underworld. I pulled myself together and tried to approach the problem analytically. First, I took stock of my water and food supply and calculated how long I might survive with what I had. One week at most. Perhaps ten days as half a corpse, I had to admit. Would they start to react to my absence at headquarters within this time? Hardly. My colleagues would start searching for me at the very moment my body was beginning to get mummified. I was surprised at my black sense of humor.

So I looked at the situation from a different angle: the breakdown. It must have been possible to fix it somehow. The problem was that I was anything but a competent motor mechanic. Still, I could try to slip under the hood of this supposedly breakdown free, bloody four-wheel-drive to repair it with the help of a screwdriver. There was an owner's manual in the glove compartment, after all.

Third angle: the *Targi*. Despite his death wish, he surely knew how to survive in the middle of nowhere at fifty degrees. Also, there had to be other Smurfs like him around somewhere in the area, for he had arrived here on foot. He might gracefully condescend to postpone his death and accompany me to his tribe, his *smala*, to allow me to pursue my way in the world of the living.

Now I had to set my priorities. First the engine, I decided. The Tuareg could wait. He wasn't doing anything but wait anyway, and that with a great deal of expertise. The siesta or *gaila* in the shade of the acacia didn't seem to hold any mysteries for him. So, I sat down under the tree and studied the owner's manual of the Land Rover, especially the chapter entitled "Possible Breakdowns." Then I ventured to confront the boiling heat, burned my hands when I opened the hood and began to fumble around with the cables and tubes. But the longer I studied the manual, the more confused I was. I felt like an anthropologist who had to perform open heart surgery on a live human patient. I was familiar with the species "automobile" and the subspecies "Land Rover" as well as their technical data, but when it came to the interior workings, I was as ill at ease as a young bridegroom faced with his first piece of furniture from Ikea.

The Targi watched with an expression of incomprehension in his eyes.

"You should wait," he said dryly.

"Wait?" I replied with irritation. "Whatever for? For death, like you?"

He shook his head.

"For *l'egedel en tafuk*," he said, "for sunset. If you continue to sweat like that in this heat, even the water of a *wadi* in torrential rain won't be able to save you."

At first, I continued to grope about for a short while, but when little stars began to dance in front of my eyes, I returned to the acacia and slid down to the bottom of its trunk.

"This is what happens to people who can't master their means of transport," he remarked.

I was too exhausted to contradict him.

"We should have a cup of tea," Meddur said.

"And wait," I added unintentionally in my head.

I was surprised to find—was it the soothing presence of the old nomad or the contact of my back with the acacia?—that I was overcome by a certain sense of equanimity. With the ongoing tea ceremony, I became sleepy, until I succumbed to the *gaila* and drowsed on like a varan at sunrise.

When, sometime later, I opened my eyes again and squinted into the setting sun, I saw the figure of the Targi bent over the engine compartment of the Land Rover. At first I guessed he was about to perform some mysterious incantation ritual to heal the car. But his precise gestures seemed to have some concrete purpose. He was actually tinkering under the hood with a screwdriver and a pair of pliers. The opened kit from which he got one tool after another lay on the ground at his feet. At last, he got behind the wheel and turned the ignition key. The engine sprang to life immediately. I hardly trusted my eyes and ears. If I had been about to write a novel, such a scenario would certainly not have come to my mind.

"Here you are," the desert mechanic said. "Now you can get in and drive back to life." I felt like a shadow in the world of the dead who is offered a boat in Hades to row back to the other side of the Styx. "If you drive through the whole night, you should reach Agadez around noon tomorrow." It only remained for him to give me a weather and road report by telling me that the night was going to be clear and there were no congestions expected along the route.

"I would have expected you to chase away the evil spirits in the engine by some magic ritual," I said, clumsily attempting to cover up my puzzlement with a doubtful quip.

"That's what I tried first," he replied, smiling. "But sometimes plan B turns out to be more effective."

Unable to utter another word, I gave him a hug and drove off. The sense of relief made me cheer out aloud. Life had me back! In the far distance, the happy activities of civilization were beckoning. Already, an ice-cold bottle of Coke popped up in front of my mental vision, with cold drops running down its side, just like in the commercials on TV.

But as I was driving on, I felt that there was a missing piece in this puzzle. The impression grew in me that I had missed out on something very basic and fundamental. Okay, I was sorry that the Targi was going to perish alone in the desert, even though that was his wish. After all, he had saved my life. But that wasn't what my unease was about. There was something else, something quite unfathomable. I had the unpleasant feeling of having missed something important in the midst of the joy of my deliverance.

Despite the reluctance to return to the place of my narrowly avoided death, I turned about abruptly after some fifty kilometers and drove back the way I had come. Initially I feared I might miss the lonely tree, but with the help of the electronic devices on board I easily found the exact spot again in the growing dusk. True, there weren't so many trees in the area that could be mistaken for my particular acacia.

I was hoping that the Targi hadn't been abducted by the *Kel Assuf* yet. But no. He was still squatting at the foot of the tree and did not seem surprised by my reappearance.

Second Night

"I EXPECTED YOU TO COME back," Meddur said by way of a greeting.

"Why?"

"You have forgotten to ask a question."

"True, that I have indeed. So: How come a man who has spent most of his life in the desert is able to repair a broken-down car engine just like that?"

"Not the engine, only the ignition."

"*Peu importe*, it doesn't matter."

"That is going to be quite a long story. Have you got time?"

"For a good story? Always. But what about you? Have you got enough time left?"

"Death is as patient as the desert. It's used to waiting. Let us have a cup of tea together so that the telling will flow more easily from my tongue. Have you got sugar? Mine has all gone."

I fetched the sugar and we sat down to tea again. That's how I learned the most unbelievable and crazy story that ever happened in the *Ténéré*, and that really means something.

But this time I wasn't going to be satisfied by losing the words in the sand without a trace. I wanted to take away something more concrete with me, for one's memory can be very tricky.

"Would you mind if I recorded your story with my tape recorder, to write it down later?" I asked Meddur. At first, he wasn't happy, but I persisted. Up to the third cup of tea, he obstinately refused the idea. He said words were not meant to be caught on paper. Words had to be like the wind. Like the Scirocco, which carries sand, smells, and sometimes clouds, they had to carry sounds, ideas, and dreams over the dunes. After which they were meant to fall back into silence to become one with the Sahara again.

I objected. I told him that the word could never be taken into custody. Not on paper and not in a human throat. That the written word could have several lives, that it could blossom out and flourish like an *achab* bush after a shower. Because it was like a seed lying fallow and waiting for a human consciousness, as the thirsty soil was waiting for the heavenly water.

He was still unwilling. He said his memories were like live beings sprung from his soul. Only the living word could carry them into the soul of the community, into the head and the mouth of his descendants where they would live on.

I answered that life was not contained in the sign itself, but in its spirit, which would remain free as long as human beings in this world would hope and love, and I quoted from Rûmi from memory: "Forms are like beakers. Their only value lies in the thirst-quenching content which flows through them."

This got him thinking. After hesitating for a while, he at last agreed, for he was eager to tell me his promised story in all its details before he was called up by Allah. And if it was going to leave a trail behind, that wouldn't be so bad after all. It couldn't hurt him anyway if there was some monkey business being played with it later. He added that what he was about to tell me had changed his own existence fundamentally. To him, it meant more than his life, because it had been so moving and unique. Therefore, he allowed me—for God's sake—to record his words and write them down, if it meant so much to me, *inshallah*.

I fetched a kerosene lamp from the car, hung it to a branch and lit it. When we had made ourselves comfortable for the night, Meddur snuggled into the glow of the hazy lamp- light and began to tell his story. He did it the African way, of course, which meant reaching out far afield and with lots of digressions, for which he apologized in advance. To set the mood, he ventured onto the branches of a strange theory on the art of storytelling.

"Maybe, the oasis of my narrative only exists in the world of my imagination and not in the outer reality," he began. "Maybe, I'm inventing a reality because a good story always contains a great deal more truth than reality."

Hey, my mind jumped right after the first two sentences. Was I listening to Noam Chomsky or to an old Targi?

But this was only the beginning of a discourse that I would never have expected from a nomad under a palaver tree.

After having sipped at his cup Meddur continued:

"Maybe, we often experience what happens to us humans through the story that we invent around it in our heads at the same time. It may be that we are the main character in a story which bends reality at its will. Anyway, I have most certainly not invented the best of all stories that I am carrying in my mind, because I still can't believe it myself. With this story, reality has disclaimed my theory. It may be, after all, that reality is nearer the truth than even the best story.

"Anyway, when we came back from the city to the desert with our new and heterogeneous clan, I first became a teacher and a *griot*, a storyteller. Later, having beaten all my opponents in poetry competitions, I became the clan's *Amghar*.

"Why it's always the best storyteller who is elected *Amghar* is clear. Coherence, collaboration, and development of any human community are based on a narrative, a common myth believed by everyone. Only when all the members believe the same narrative and share the same dreams and values, they can also speak the same language and pull on the same rope. It is only by means of the word that several individuals can become a group, a community, a society, and something like continuity can develop. Only through the word can a person survive as a civilized being.

"Now, it was useful to convey basic values like *tekarakit* and *asshak* by recitation of stories, it was fascinating to liberate my spirit by the sound of my words and to maintain the content of my culture in public performances and by constant repetition. I enjoyed bringing to life my people's *tesawit*, the heroic stories, in ever more brilliant forms. I became a master of the *tangalen*, the so-called "Speech through the flower," and danced around the unspeakable on ever wilder artful allusions. When I was lonely, I entered fiery dialogues with my inner demon, that hairy, smirking goblin with his red eyes who stinks like a ram and still torments me with his aggressive outbursts. Often, too, I spoke to my camel, who absorbed my words and quietly chewed on them.

"But an outstanding storyteller cannot be satisfied with that, and I yearned to become one of the greatest. I no longer found it satisfying to play superficial games and fight for the admiration of women and the favor of the public in poetry competitions. I wanted to fathom the enormous depths of the world. I yearned for even more than that, I wanted to lift my verbal art onto a higher level. I was very eager to develop the potential of the spoken word into a lasting creative power, in order to pass it on, enriched by new dimensions, to my successor. In a process similar to my life as a whole, my words should pile on top of each other while constantly changing and developing further. I was dreaming of a successive process subjected to constant simultaneity. In my words, the physical and the temporal dimensions were to merge into an unfathomable space. Thus, I really became an *Amghar*."

I was stupefied. While he was talking, there arose before my inner eye a puzzling incompatibility, a kind of oral palimpsest in which, instead of written words, there were sounds, echoes, ideas and mental images that shone through and enriched one another beyond time and space.

"As an explorer in the fantasy world, I wanted to be able to dream up and express all the secrets that are hidden behind the things of the real world. This is how I became a conjuror, a shaman. I learned to master the language of the hereafter. In transmitting my visions to my audience, I delivered their existence of its monotony and dreariness. I overlaid their naked reality with the golden brocade gown of fantasy. A good *Amghar* makes the world more bearable, he places the events in their context, he creates meaning and order."

I couldn't hold back the remark that up there in the north, in the civilized world of the *Ikufar*, the *Amghar* also tell the people stories. However, since they don't believe in them, they make nobody dream.

These words produced a smile on Meddur's face.

"The greatest nightmare doesn't lie in the monsters and catastrophes that we imagine but in the emptiness of feigned dreams. A dream is only a dream when it is free. As soon as it becomes a means to an end, it loses its healing power. This always takes vengeance, for who betrays his dreams loses his soul."

I nodded silently and ruminated over his words.

In the following silence, the Targi seemed to draw his spiritual breath to come to his story at last.

"I am not going to mention the place names that play a role in my story, for names are of the devil. They used to be gifts of God. Today, they are no longer. Out there is a world moving closer and closer, a world in which people who are possessed by the devil suck up the names and drain them like a passion fruit, leaving only the empty husk. Hollow names are the graves of the soul. I have to protect the places in my narrative, lest they get destroyed. That's why I will not name them, for names and geographical indications attract evil spirits. Only as nobodies in a no-man's-land can men such as me survive. Only where no one can hurt anyone else are we protected. The more invisible we are, the better Allah will take care of us. And the better Allah takes care of us, the more invisible we are for his crazy warriors and the money hunters who pay them. Here in the desert, on the threshold to the unbearable, the limits that people have set themselves are insubstantial. Our only limitations are sand, wind and horizon. And each of these is boundless. Only infinity sets us limits. Against that, even the most ambitious bureaucracy is powerless. Who can prevent the shifting dunes from crossing and effacing borders? Who can arrest the wind that smuggles the sand across roadblocks and tollgates? For this reason, we are people of the wind. The wind sets us free."

Even though I found that he was pushing the romantic aspect of nomadic life a little too far, I couldn't ward off a certain wistfulness. Somewhere in my heart his words struck a chord that I hadn't expected there.

"The location of the beginning of my story is nowhere and everywhere. The *ikufar* might try to describe it with names like Libya, Niger, Mali, or Chad in order to be able to find it again. Not for me since I am on my way to a nameless dimension from which there is no coming back.

"Anyway, on our return from Agadez we had discovered a completely remote valley in the promontory of a *gam*, a table mountain, in which there grew a few low bushes and three palm trees. That was a sign of an *atankor*, a waterhole with groundwater within reach. We dug, and not very deep below the surface we found enough water to feed a well. So, we pitched our tents and huts and erected *zeribas* to fence in our animals. A half-grown acacia was declared our palaver tree. Protected and threatened as well by the desert, we attempted to regain that free life whose memory had haunted us again and again in the city.

"The first years were hard. We found it difficult to complete the circles of survival that made our life at the bosom of the void possible. Some gave up and traveled back south to the abundance that had drained us. But most of us stayed. Like the sand settles again after a *harmattan's* dusty breath, the restlessness in our hearts died down. Like the varan adapts to the dryness of his environment, we accustomed ourselves to life in the desert again and became one with it. After a few months we were able to regain our inner richness out of our material shortage, and on the strength of this inner richness we managed to govern the material shortage. We dropped the routines of city life just as the snake sheds its skin, and through the balance that we regained, we found our way back to a precarious happiness.

"Gradually the circles of our wanderings widened. The more familiar we became with the desert, the deeper we ventured into it and even beyond it. Our senses were sharpened again. The old reflexes that we had believed to be dead awakened to life. Again, we became experienced gatherers, hunters, shepherds, and tradesmen like our ancestors. Unfortunately, Allah brought us another trial with the second great drought extending from 1983 to 1984. The water in the well sank as our demand for it increased. We were forced to consider a shift of our *duar*, our nomadic tent village, although we couldn't find an alternative location within reach. The well-known oases were occupied already, and to find new ones was impossible in the face of the drought. After long ruminations and deliberations, we decided to approach the Sahel in the south again, where vegetation and water supply were somewhat more abundant."

The Targi sipped his tea and brooded.

"Water means nothing as long as you have enough of it," he said and made another pause, which tested my patience considerably.

"But then he showed up. An utterly surreal appearance. At first, we only heard a distant rumbling, which was rapidly approaching and eventually grew to deafening dimensions, more frightful than a wild swarm of hornets. We looked at each other in amazement. A sort of monster of gleaming metal, as we had never seen even in Agadez, was arising from the horizon. The monster moved up to within a few meters close to our *duar*, which seemed to shrink involuntarily in the face of his bulk, before it turned right and came to a halt with its side facing us. We stood gaping open-mouthed. Some men grasped their weapons. The women took the children and disappeared behind the *gam*. As for myself, I stood at the front of our crowd and admired the giant vehicle with its rounded rear end. How this giant metal camel without humps had found its way to us mystified all of us.

"After the monster had finished gasping and wheezing, the door of its cabin opened. A weird human being climbed down, jumped into the sand, and looked in our direction.

"The man appeared like a demon to us. Insecure, we all stepped back a pace. The tall, bearded, and longhaired visitor did not seem to mind. If it hadn't been for his dark sunglasses, he could have been taken for a reincarnation of St. John the Baptist, whom we call *Yahya*. His beard and hair were of a golden hue and his skin was as red as the eastern sky at the time of sunrise. When he stepped towards us, we retreated even further. The man shrugged his shoulders and returned to his truck where he cowered down in its shade. He was clad in an oil stained pair of dungarees and a grey T-shirt with holes in it. His feet stuck in leather military boots.

"Nothing happened for an hour. After all, it was *takellawt*, which was a good excuse for passivity. So great was my fascination for the strange apparition that I didn't grow tired. As soon as the murmurings of the villagers behind me had ebbed down and they had gradually retreated to their *gaila* under some shade or other, I carefully approached the stranger. When I stood before him, he took off his sunglasses and looked up at me. At first, he had to blink because of the glare of the sun, but after some time his gaze became firm. I had never seen such blue eyes. It was as if two deep lakes were looking at me.

"'*Assalamu Alaykum,*' he said and lifted his hand in greeting.

"'*Assalam.*'

"Insecure, I shifted my weight from one foot to the other.

"'*Assieds-toi,*' he invited me in French, and it seemed to me that pebbles were rolling through his voice, so peculiar was his pronunciation.

"'I'm not French,' he said when he registered the mystification in my face. 'I come from a small country next to France where another language is mostly spoken besides French.'

"I nodded as if I knew and sat down.

"'Are you thirsty?' he asked and offered me a flask.

"I took a big gulp from it. And another one.

"'By the *imzad* of the loved ones, the water is good,' I said knowingly.

"'In the cistern behind me I have fifteen cubic meters of it. That is 15,000 liters.'

"'I see,' I said and probably drew an uncomprehending face because I couldn't quite grasp such big figures.

"'That's a lot of water,' he said. 'How many people are there in your clan? Forty? Fifty? Let's say fifty. Since your bodies are genetically conditioned to need relatively small amounts of water, your clan could survive for about 150 days on the content of the cistern. Including your animals in the calculation we would still get a month and a half.'

"This, I could grasp.

"'That's a lot of water indeed,' I said, 'and water is very precious. But we cannot buy any because we have no money. Except you would take a goat for it.'

"'Who is talking of payment?' said the man. 'I give you all that water as a present.'

"'What? The whole cistern? You can't be serious?'

"'Sure I am! I have made it my duty to bring water to people in need with that cistern truck that I have built myself. Look here!', he said, knocked the sand from his pants and stepped up to the cabin door. 'Can you see those marks? There are exactly seventy-one.

That's the number of people whose lives I've saved with my water. Other men carve a notch in their rifle butt or paint black stripes on the nose of their fighter jet to keep a record of their victims. As for me, I keep a record of the survivors.'

"We sat down again.

"'So, you drive crisscross through the desert with your monster truck in order to save men from dying of thirst?'

"'Exactly! Because I want to cross the devil.'

"'I see!'"

The Targi looked meaningfully at me.

"Nothing was clear, but to cross the devil couldn't be amiss, could it?"

I nodded silently.

"Well, I got talking to the man and I learned from him that he was called Jonas Brunner. He said his name was almost an obligation since it was the same as the German word for a well or a fountain. And his first name was taken from the story of Yunus from the Sura *as-Saffat*, who is swallowed by a big fish and spat out again and thrown onto the beach. He called the prophet Jonah and the fish whale. Besides the fact that the man really seemed to be like a fish that got lost in the desert, the reference was not clear to me at first. Concerning the second part of his name, his explanation was obvious: When a man is called "Well Man" or "Fountain Man" or something like that, it is no wonder that he should travel through the desert with a mobile fountain. To me, the big vehicle from which he had crawled out appeared rather like the big fish from the Sura. Anyway, Jonas Brunner with his cistern in the glowing heat had something watery about him, which made me give him the nickname of *ad- dalw*.

"'*ad-dalw*,' asked the stranger, 'what does that mean?'

"'Waterman.' "

"That seemed to surprise and amuse him.

"'By the beard of the Prophet, that's my star sign.'

"'Your star sign?'

"'Yes, I was born under the sign of Aquarius, which means Waterman.'"

At these words, the Targi's eyes looked intensively at me from the shade of his head gear: "Since I can only recognize varying shapes of the camel in the night sky, as you know, what the man told me of his star sign only appeared mysterious. But the name of Waterman stuck to him because it suited his mobile cistern, his eyes, and his activity. Later I learned that the small country of his origin consisted almost exclusively of vertical deserts of ice and snow. The mountains were a lot higher and colder than the tops of the *Aïr* and the *Ahaggar*. Storms there didn't carry sand but snowflakes, were called avalanches and were mostly caused by humans themselves, which seemed odd. At the time, I just couldn't believe that natural phenomena could be caused by humans. As for myself, I had never seen a man launch a *samum*, which we call "poison wind." Only Allah can blow it, otherwise there wouldn't be the fatality of the *kismet* anymore, but only coincidence. Anyway, I got the impression that the poor man had fallen from a cold inferno into a hot one, and to judge from his red and peeled cheeks he wasn't suited for it."

Meddur took a sip of tea to clear his hoarse voice and continued.

"I asked him why he had come to the desert. He replied that was because of his profession. He was an engineer, and he was building infrastructures for large companies.

"'What sort of infrastructures?' I asked.

"'I am something like a builder of pyramids,' he said, without considering the fact that I was a Targi and had never heard of pyramids before meeting him and knew even less about them than I knew about Exxon or Mobil.

"'I see. But now you have become a nomad just like us, only that you carry admittedly good, but dead water with you.'

"'Dead water?'

"'It is imprisoned in the belly of your metal demon and cannot flow freely.'

"'It's not much different from your camels here. Only, they don't yield the two hundred liters that they drink within ten minutes.'

"'They transform it into the movement on which the Tuareg ride through the desert.'

"'And I just roll on my water instead of riding on it. Where is the difference?'

"'Your monster isn't driven by water, that's why it is dead, and so is the water in it. And what emerges at the back stinks.'

"'And that's not the case with your camels?' he answered, amused.

"On that, I had to agree with him. But the bad smell of the camel was the price to pay to ride on free, living waters.

"'At least my camel's smell doesn't dye the sky grey.'

"This time it was his turn to agree with me.

"It was a draw.

"The satisfaction on my face seemed to amuse him.

"Then I looked at him more closely. Most people have their character and their age written on their faces. This wasn't the case with him. I had the impression to be sitting across from a man who constantly stayed in the wrong place. Somehow, he appeared to me like the attendant from the filling station in Agadez, but without a filling station. Although he gave me the impression that he knew what he was about, he looked quite lost. Later, when I got to know him better—his reticent shy ways, his determined fighter's attitude, his wispy soul—I could fathom the effort it must have cost him to enter into conversation with me on our first encounter.

"'Why are you doing this?' I asked him.

"'To help people.'

"'I don't mean that. What are you looking for by doing this?'

"He looked at me quite puzzled, probably because he hadn't expected this question. He didn't know anything about my calling, and he couldn't know that as a shaman I was blessed with the deep vision that can read people's souls.

"Waterman hesitated with his reply.

"'I am looking for life, and life is water.'

"'But life and water evaporate.'

"He nodded. 'I'm afraid they do.'

"'Then find the source.'

"'I carry it with me.'

"'A source that isn't connected with the earth isn't a source.'

"He considered these words for a while before answering: 'I have found a source, a spring, far in the north, among warped derricks in the middle of a defunct oilfield. That's where I can always refill my cistern to bring water to the people. With this water you could grow millet and cultivate date palms even in this barren ground.'

"'A Targi's garden is the back of his camel,' I replied, feeling quite poetic.

'But even your camel needs pastures and water to survive. And you with it.'

"There he was right.

"'Talk to the others,' he said. 'Obviously, you don't lack the necessary assertiveness and rhetoric skills. Convince them to accept my offer. I don't want any money for it, I only want to make life easier for you.'

"I looked at him critically. This Jonas seemed to be a real piece of work. No wonder, given his attitude, he was forced to whizz around the desert as a lonely man like a black beetle gone crazy. But I was somehow touched by him. I assumed a deep rift in his soul, a badly patched up fragility. He was a boundary walker between two deserts, an inner and an outer desert. I felt that this man's soul harbored a secret that I wanted to uncover. That's why the man had to stay. So, I decided to convince my kinfolks that dead water could also be beneficial to life.

"I nodded to *ad-dalw* and went back to the tents. The time of the *gaila* being over by now, my clansmen immediately crowded around me to learn what I had found out.

"I broadly explained to them who the man was and what it was all about.

"When I had come to the end of my report, there arose a muddled murmuring. Some said that was witchcraft. The truck had apparently come from the *Tikdabra*, where there could be no water. Others warned of the treachery of the Europeans, who in the past had only sown discord among the tribes. This foreigner was just another example of their strange attitude to the world and to life. They were only slaves who constantly spoke of freedom but really carried a prison in their hearts and wanted to jail everybody in it. Another one finally added that we hadn't left the modern world behind only to be caught up by it again at the first opportunity.

"Apparently, my task wasn't going to be as easy as expected.

"When the murmurings had quieted down a little, I began to speak again by turning around the argument of the last critical speaker: 'Bismillah'—in Allah's name—which is better: to be caught up by the modern world or to have to crawl back to it?'

"That did the trick. Like every argument which shows that there's no real choice because things will turn out the same anyway.

"However, my clansmen continued to grumble. Their aversion against the world represented by this foreigner was too deep, and their fear of the metal monster with its strange driver was too great. I had to add a stronger, more sacred argument if I wanted to turn their minds around for good.

"'True, he is a foreigner,' I began again, 'but why should hospitality be practiced only towards those born with sand in their eyes? Do you really want to violate the unwritten law of hospitality only because you don't like the visitor? You know that every guest is invited by Allah and that we have received everything we own from Allah and are therefore obliged to share it with the guest sent by Allah, as if he were Allah himself. What is worse: to lose your soul or to open your tents for an unpleasant man? As for myself, I will certainly welcome him to my tent, if you don't object.'

"That sank in. They threw a last distrustful glance at the truck and the cowering figure in front of it, shrugged their shoulders and went about their business. And I invited Waterman to tea in my tent.

"You have experienced it yourself," Meddur commented on his narrative, "that the unwritten law of hospitality is a question of survival. But only if everybody sticks to it." He pulled the blanket around his shoulders. "Are you tired, my friend? Do you want me to stop for today?" he asked. I said no. For who would stop on the threshold to a panopticon whose figures were about to come to life? Besides, my Targi was no Sherazad and I was no Sultan. After a short pause, he continued.

"So, Waterman stayed in our *duar*. At first, people avoided him. But when he began to dispense water from his cistern to fill up the water containers of the members of my family, the other families first sent their children to get some drops of the precious liquid, too. Later, they came themselves. After a week, the discreet and silent stranger belonged to the clan like every other man and every camel of the *duar*, and his truck seemed to have merged with the landscape like the rocks of the *gam* in the distance. Except that the *gam*, in contrast to the cistern truck, couldn't be milked as if it were a camel mare.

"Since time does not exist in the desert, I had enough time to observe Waterman more closely. Even in the greatest heat he didn't seem to stay put. He was constantly busy fixing or repairing something, as if he was unable to restrain his hands from their urge to move. It seemed to me that he wanted to seal Allah's world to make sure nothing was lost.

"Gradually I came to understand that he wasn't only a stranger to us, but also to the world and life at large. Even daylight seemed to lose itself in him. That's why there was this strange wisp in his eyes.

"One day I asked him why there were so many clouds passing through his gaze when the sky above was blue and motionless.

"'The sky is one thing, man is another,' was his answer.

"I scrutinized the sky above and was confronted with the same infinity as in my soul. One was reflected in the other. What a strange attitude to life this Waterman seemed to have!

"Initially, he slept in our tent, where he first frightened my wife and children, until they realized that he wasn't so peculiar as he seemed, after all. But a trace of distrust remained. Later I got him a tent of his own, in which he was free to wallow through his nightmares without disturbing anyone.

"Although I couldn't really understand him as a human being, in due course we became more familiar with each other. At the same time, I felt a growing fascination for this strange being which had come from an enigmatic world beyond the desert where things moved of their own and even flew in the sky. He represented a cornucopia for my insatiable thirst for knowledge.

"As for him, he got to know our ways and found true pleasure in our manners and traditions, and he was especially fond of our mystic interpretation of the *Qur'an*, which was enriched by spirits haunting the desert.

"He had a special liking for our *tagelmust*, our turban like veil, which he soon tied around his own head like an experienced *imohar*. The contrast thus created to his dungarees and military boots gave him a bizarre look. He found it most peculiar that our women didn't veil their faces like Arab women, but our men did.

"I explained to him that this was a question of identity.

"'The *tagelmust* makes the *imohar*. It makes a young man into a warrior. By the way the veil is worn it expresses something and becomes a carrier of meaning.'

"'So you veil yourselves to reveal yourselves,' he said, slightly amused.

"'The cover makes the fullness,' I replied. 'Emptiness doesn't need a veil.'

"He scratched his beard and murmured something about some German philosopher who had said a similar thing.

"I explained to him that the world consisted of two spheres: the hot one and the cold one. This was also demonstrated by the desert, which was scorching hot by day and ice cold by night. Our body apertures, for example, belonged to the cold sphere. Evil spirits could slip in, especially through our breath. The *tagelmust* was a protection against that. It was a kind of "Guardian of Order" and a safeguard against the evil eye. Without his veil, the *imohar* stood naked in the face of Allah, the owner of our breath, *emeli n unfas.*

"'In my case, it protects me mainly from the sun,' said Waterman, whose face was no longer peeling like an old tree-bark ever since he had been wearing a veil. He always saw the practical side of things first. Even though spiritual and religious matters interested him very much, he couldn't see much more than cultural idiosyncrasies and exotic expressions in them.

"I tried to convince him of the profundity of the world and to convert him to a spiritual belief, but he remained a man of figures and technical challenges.

"When I told him that God spoke to humanity mainly in the desert because, due to the silence, He could more likely be heard there, he answered that a man who wanted to hear God could hear Him everywhere, while the deaf man remained deaf also in the desert.

"'Just as you do,' I pertly replied.

"'That's right. Where you can feel Allah's breath, I can only hear the wind. I just see the sand running down from the permanent dune while you are interested in the hard core beneath it, in which you detect God's everlasting presence behind the fleetingness of human hustle and bustle. For you, there is a divine realm and a world on and beneath the earth, for me there's only reality and nothing else. Where you see demons and gods, I see natural forces. Where I see mountains, you see spiritual temples. Despite that difference, as human beings, we live in the same world, and we face the same problems. Whether everything is over with death, or our soul only leaves our body after seven years, as you believe, who cares? In the end, everything goes bust anyway.'

"After such diatribes, which were rare with him, he usually turned away and didn't utter another word for days.

"No doubt, he belonged to the cold sphere, though he sometimes heated up for a short time.

"His fetish was his truck with all its technical gadgets. His talisman consisted of his pliers, his screwdriver, and his computer.

"He found it amusing that we *imohar* never place our amulets on the ground, so that it can't be taken over by evil spirits. He found it interesting that we always stick our sword in the sand with its hilt down. But the deeper sense of such actions remained hidden from him. That's why he saw it as a waste when we didn't consume the milk that remained in the animals' udders overnight but buried it in the ground.

"Humans, who were created by Allah from clay and divine breath, were for him the result of a long process of evolution in which monkeys had become human beings. The art of healing for him consisted of science and pharmaceuticals, while for us it encompasses religion, magic, music and the application of efficacious plants and herbs. In his world, happy coincidences had no reason behind them, certainly not God's blessing. So, there was no salvation in his understanding of the world, but only the fateful entanglement of cause and effect.

"I couldn't understand what sense it made for him to think that way, for it didn't make him happy. However, at his side I learned a great deal about the mental set up of those who only know of a here and now. Given his belief that everything was futile anyway, I was puzzled by his manic effort to save human lives, to give away water and to help our tribe. This incoherence was the lever with which I could deconstruct his mental framework when it was trying to build itself around my thoughts like a grid.

"The only point on which we more or less agreed concerned the end of the world. He, too, could see a phase approaching in which all living beings would eventually kill each other. In his world view, too, the sun would eventually become pure light in a cosmic explosion, and in his understanding, too, everything would in the end disintegrate to dust, to nothing at all.

"However, we disagreed about what was going to happen after that. For him, there was nothing left after the universe—including the icy center of hell in its fire spitting volcano—had burnt up completely. He shook his head uncomprehendingly when I told him about the demon *In-Tazat*—the devil's representative—who would then come to seduce humanity. For him, there was no "Doomsday" in the *Gehenna,* no "Lake of Fire" with the Prophets to the left of God's throne, where the evil souls like the hagglers and the cattle thieves would be punished. He thought nothing of the resurrection of the good souls into Paradise. The world's fate for him was a sinking back into the nothingness from which it had come. I could paint Paradise in the most brilliant colors for him, he just didn't believe in a hereafter, in which ever green acacias offer abundant shade to the *gaila* and the wells are full to the brim even in the dry season.

"He didn't believe in protective angels either, although he appeared to me more and more like one himself. In short, he was educated, intelligent, humane, and determined—and yet he didn't understand anything of the world.

"By contrast, what he was very knowledgeable about was the technical world.

"In just a few months he transformed our *duar* into a high tech oasis. It began with the water, the basic need for our lives on the edge of the habitable world. Since he usually took about a week to refill his empty cistern from his distant source, he fetched an excavator and other equipment from some store only known to him, and with the help of some of our young men he rebuilt our well so that it offered an easier access to the dwindling ground water. Finally, he added a watertight reservoir that he could always refill from his truck, thus bridging over the water supply during his absences. From various stores he had set up in the caves of the *Aïr* and *Ahaggar* he always fetched materials to ensure our lives on the fringe of the desert despite the terrible drought, while there was great hardship in other areas of the Sahel. It remained a mystery to me where he could always procure all those tools and machines as well as the oil and fuel resources for which he established a store in our *duar*. Out of principle, he never answered my questions on that score.

"He erected some solar panels, which allowed us not only to prolong our days and to make our cold nights more bearable, but even to grind our millet in a sort of mill. He built houses and sheds from stone, like the ones in the city, he laid out gardens and planted trees, especially date palms, and he tried to convince the reluctant gatherers and hunters of the advantages of agriculture and the keeping of stores for provisions. The young ones were willing to help him, while the old timers still opposed his ideas. But we all profited from this strange man and his tremendous determination, talents and visions. Even older people gradually took to wearing sunglasses under the glaring sun.

"I became his right hand and more and more often accompanied him on his wanderings. He patiently explained to me the electronics in his truck, he taught me to drive the vehicle and to handle the caterpillar he always took with him, familiarized me with the GPS, sondes, radar, and radio, he showed me how to set up and adjust a parabolic antenna and to set up and program various other gadgets—in short—I became the extension of his right arm.

"I remember that he had stuck a picture of a great blue dune on his dashboard.

"'That isn't a dune, it's a wave,' he explained. 'A picture by a Japanese painter called Hokusai.'

"'A wave?'

"'Yes, it doesn't consist of sand but of water. In the Pacific Ocean—that's a kind of watery desert—such waves can grow up to thirty meters.'

"I found it amazing to learn that water could take that kind of shapes naturally and water dunes could reach such sizes.

"He sometimes listened to music in his cabin. That was very strange because it surrounded one like a room full of vibrations. But also because he didn't need any sound recordings. His music seemed to come from outer space.

"One day, I showed him the old spring-driven gramophone that I had originally gotten from Agadez. I had only three records left for it after two had been broken during our trek north. One of them played the music of a man called Glenn Miller, another that of Louis Armstrong, and on the third the label had become illegible, but someone from the city had told me that the music was from a man called Beethoven, who had attempted to catch the voice of fate itself. This was my favorite record, for it suited the English inscription on its casing, of which the trader who had sold it to me had said that it meant "His Master's Voice". I cranked up some music. Papapapam.

"Waterman said the appliance was from the Stone Age and a real catastrophe in terms of sound quality. I replied that I preferred my music appliance to his big music that came from nowhere. Uncomprehendingly, he shook his head.

"'Look here,' I said to him and pointed at the needle on the shellac record, 'these are the furrows of life, the grooves of our journey from birth to death. They strive towards the center in which are located the spirit and the hearts of people. That is why there is written the musician's name. Like our lives, the needle wears itself out. Sometimes scratches occur and the master's voice gets a click, that's when a believer doubts Allah's power, which is a great betrayal. However, what is much more important: This record has a beginning and an end, and it is unique like every human being on earth; Your music has no body, no substance. It plays on and on unless somebody stops it, and it is the same for everyone and everywhere because it is too perfect. It rebels against the unwritten laws of nature. It detaches itself from life. It is nothing but an escape from reality, an act of treason against life. Voilà!'

"'You may look at it like that,' Waterman said dryly. 'But if that'—he pointed at the gramophone—'is supposed to be your master's voice, then Allah seems to suffer from a sore throat.'

"Again, he couldn't understand anything. And why couldn't he understand? Because he was a perfectionist, a *homo faber*, as he called himself again and again, a man who leaves nothing to chance, always plans everything and wants to keep everything under control.

"'You can do as you like,' I said to him one day, 'but you cannot plan your destiny and you can't predict it. *Kismet* lies in Allah's hands.'

"At this, he smiled meaningfully.

"'I have developed an effective remedy against that.'

"'It's impossible. There is no remedy against destiny. What has to happen will happen, whatever you do. Like the story of the gardener who sees death in the sultan's garden in Damascus and rides off on his master's fastest horse to escape from it into Egypt. But it is preordained that death will be waiting for him on his arrival in Cairo.'

"'That's why it is important to apply my remedy, which consists in always reserving a plan B.'

"'A plan B?'

"'Exactly. You are right when you say that chance sometimes plays bad tricks on you. This must be part of the plan to avoid being outwitted by the unforeseeable. And that's what you need a plan B for.'

"'And when destiny also crosses your plan B?'

"'Then I will apply plan B's plan B, which can also be seen as plan C. That's like the Russian doll in my truck cabin that fascinates you. As soon as you open one of the dolls the next one appears, and so on and on. Analogous to those dolls, there is always a plan B in every situation in life, if only you have enough imagination and look ahead a certain distance.'

"'Plan B is also ordained by Allah.'

"'That's what YOU pretend, but there is no proof for it.'

"'Yes, there is,' I said, hardly being able to suppress my sense of triumph. 'In the end, there isn't another doll in the last doll, only divine emptiness.'

"He couldn't say anything to that. His eyes seemed to lose themselves in a hazy mental distance. He stood up and left the tent without a word.

"Still, I had to admit that he had a solution for every problem indeed. He appeared to me like a magician. Whenever there was a difficulty of some sort, he said: 'Not to despair, just ask Jonas,' and solved the problem. Another of his favorite phrases was: 'If there is a need for something, just build it.'

"In view of his unflagging building activities, soon there was nothing left to build. We lived like kings in a magic garden and wondered when fate would present us with its bill for it.

"But perhaps *ad-dalw* was a guardian angel sent by Allah, watching over us. That's why he never slept at night but fumbled around with various things in the glow of his self-made light. 'Sleep is a waste of time,' he used to say, or: 'life is too short to be slept through.' Sometimes, he strolled about between the dunes at night, driven by unrest, some inner gramophone spring, seeming neither to seek nor to find anything.

"Though rarely smiling, he sometimes said particularly droll things.

"For example, one day he declared out of the blue that he had missed his life, for his true talent would have been in the turning over of sun roasting female tourists with a meat fork. As we imagined that, we shook with laughter.

"Or he came up with new phrases, which went round immediately and were taken up by our young people. One of these was: 'Who shits into the thistles needs a tough ass.' Another phrase gave a strange reason for fighting: 'When shots are fired, boredom dies first,' he declared laconically.

"But he could also be very acrimonious: 'In my former world, it is more lucrative to look clever than to be clever,' he commented, for instance.

"At the end of my apprenticeship with him, Waterman gave me a present which I have never put down since and which I am still carrying with me."

Meddur retrieved from the folds of his gown a classic red Swiss pocketknife with a white cross on it and showed it to me.

"'This is the smallest, most practical and essential plan B in the world,' Waterman explained to me, thus completing my apprenticeship by demonstrating what could be done with his knife. My beautifully crested dagger appeared extremely limited and primitive after that."

The night was already far advanced, but Meddur still did not appear to be tired. He set about preparing some more tea for us. I stood up to stretch my stiff limbs a little and to relax my feet. The air had become very cold. Luckily, there was no wind, for otherwise I could hardly have endured it in the open, despite my down jacket and my sleeping bag. The celestial cupola over my head with its billions of stars made me feel the woefulness of my existence in this world more heavily than ever before. At the same time, this view filled me with deep longing and hopefulness. During that night, the hardly visible crescent moon looked like a sickle that was too thin to mow the stars, for it intensified their luminosity and made the darkness around me more impenetrable. When I stepped back under the foliage of the acacia, throwing a last glance at the sky, it appeared to me as if the stars were growing on the twigs of the tree like small fireflies. The acacia seemed to carry fruits of light. In this view, I detected all the dreams and desires ever harbored by human beings in this world.

Deeply moved, I sat down again in the beam of the dim lamplight and watched Meddur as he was pouring the first round of tea and building up the froth in the cups by swaying his arm. "Dreams are like foam," I was thinking, carefully sipping the piping hot beverage.

Wordlessly, Meddur also sipped his tea for a while.

Then he continued his narrative.

"For my part, I taught Waterman how to survive in the desert without the artificial help of mechanics and technology. I showed him how to detect the treacherous quicksand, I explained to him the dangers around salt lakes, the difference between a *ghourd,* which is a star-shaped dune, a parabolic and a sickle dune and the advantage of millet over wheat. I revealed to him how to find water where there isn't any when one had to travel through the desert without the 15,000 liters of fresh water he disposed of. I took him hunting, showed him how to stalk antelopes against the wind and I taught him the virtue he had in the least degree: patience. Whoever wants to survive in the desert, I explained, had to be slow, patient, and shouldn't rush around like some racing rat chased by a desert fox, as he was doing. We practiced this for hours while waiting for an antelope at a water hole. At first, he nearly burst with impatience, but gradually his disposition quieted down and allowed him to shoot and kill his first prey animal."

Meddur turned straight to me: "You are such a driven man, too, thinking you could bypass the laws of the desert with your four-wheel-drive. But these laws will eventually overtake every individual who has tried to circumnavigate them on the sly. Because people form part of nature, carrying these laws in them. The desert requires slowness, the slowness of a chameleon. If you want to survive in the middle of the summer at the time of *la tarrut* in the *Ténéré*, you must change yourself into a lizard. You must remain absolutely calm, and fossilize yourself to be one with the eternity of the rocks. Haste will be punished. For haste needs help from outside, as you have experienced yourself. The desert requires slowness because only slowness takes its greatness into account.

"Out of respect for the infinity of the desert, we Targi have given up all concepts of time. Our patience is humility, for the desert is God's Garden, where He speaks to humankind. On top of patience, you can add what you Europeans call sustainability. A Targi will only kill one gazelle though he might get a whole herd in the sight of his gun. It's always possible to catch up with an escaping herd, but a senselessly killed animal can't be revived. To live on the edge of the possible, it is imperative not to upset the balance of nature and to apply sensible survival strategies.

"I advised Waterman, if he was ever very thirsty, to eat the raw meat of the animal just killed and to drink its blood. I showed him how to collect the morning dew so as not to die from thirst, how to dig yourself in to survive in extreme heat, and how to procure some shade without a tree or a rock.

"At last, I asked him if he knew why you couldn't find anything that stinks to heaven in the desert. Before he could come up with some scientific explanations, I held up my hands in self defense and answered him: because the dead in the desert are really dead. And because the guardians of the desert always clean up at once. Despite appearances, there is always a lot of teeming life around death in the desert. And the job will be completed to perfection. Nothing is left to rot away for months. Everything is recycled and cleaned up immediately.

"The stench in the big cities is due to the fact that there are far too many walking dead who don't know they're dead yet.

"That is how I acquainted Waterman with our people's knowledge and wisdom. And he, otherwise so impatient, to my surprise listened carefully to my words. Apparently, some of the things I told him struck a hidden chord in him. For me, that was proof of the fact that even in so called civilized humans there still lay dormant the old nomad who yearns back for a lost freedom. But it might have been only wishful thinking on my part.

"In any case, encouraged by his attention, I continued with my explanations, just as I am doing with you now, my dear Jean Tourel.

"Do you know the main difference between modern city life and life in the desert?" I shrugged my shoulders to indicate my ignorance.

"In movement and in rhythm, city life is an organized chaos of crisscrossing fast movements. Every second, something happens, something clashes with something else. No movement seems to be coordinated with another movement; everything runs hectically across one another in confusion. Every individual has objectives and pursues them with this or that other individual, often against odds. It's a dynamic of progress by leaps, breaks and changes of direction, like the zig zag course of some gazelle running away from a dog, only there is no dog running after city people since the dog is running inside of them.

"In contrast, life in the desert is best illustrated by a caravan. The word "caravan" itself is already a word with a sweeping rhythm that one can imagine as the movement of a wave. The caravan is shrouded in mystery, surrounded by the perfume of spices and exotic delicacies. Its progress through the wasteland seems to be slow, but that is deceptive, for the regularity of its movements is unstoppable and secures its timely arrival at its destination."

"Like a ship at sea," I threw in.

"Of that you are a better judge than I," said Meddur. "In any case, it is characterized by constancy and clear line management in an endless space. It sways complacently through the void and hardly ever crosses another caravan. It moves and it stops on its own. It is autonomous because it cannot expect any help from outside.

"People come and go in the desert, like everywhere in the world, but the caravan moves on into eternity like life itself."

I objected that might be all right in the desert, but people in the civilized world needed connections in order to reach each other, and such connecting lines first needed to be built.

"Caravans don't need roads," he answered, "caravans are the roads."

"In Paris or New York that road would soon come to an end," I gave him to consider.

"Because you don't build any roads but grids and networks on which you climb around like monkeys, without realizing that you are their prisoners. The caravan is free. Its road emerges under the camels' footsteps, which never lose their way because they are one with the desert, like the shifting dunes."

He fell silent. While he was pouring the second cup of tea, I was contemplating what I had heard. I could comprehend much of what he'd said, although it stood out as exotic romanticism in the context of modern civilization. My admiration for his idealized vision of the desert was fighting against the rational spirit of the industrialized world with its overdose of attractions, its areas of conflict, and its numerous, constantly changing, or concurrent temptations. I had to admit that all that led to a certain dulling effect and to a serious loss of values, which had to be compensated by morbid yearning for pleasure, entertainment, and unattainable happiness. In such a context, people are only slaves to their own senses, becoming addicted and self centered, and eventually finding themselves beyond good and evil because it is impossible to build up any form of morality on the pleasure principle.

In pure contrast to that, here in the desert a life on the edge offered itself to me, a life whose regular course provided only little variety, but which upheld such values as dignity, reliability, continuity, and modesty. Here, things didn't dance around constant overdoses of lust. Life in the desert was not about overproduction and consumption of superfluous things, but about fulfillment of basic needs.

The constantly changing kaleidoscope of artificial shapes and colors in the so called civilized world stood in contrast to the internalization of simple lines in solitude. Overdose stood against emptiness. Senselessness against meaningfulness.

I had the impression that animalistic and even bestial drives could thrive better under cover of progress than in the merciless wilderness.

When the second cup of tea was poured, Meddur began to talk about Waterman's vehicle: "*Ad-dalw's* truck was more than a vehicle, more than a mobile giant cistern with a cooling system. It was his headquarters, his emergency vehicle, his castle, his rolling workshop, and his survival kit, all in one. To a large extent, Waterman had designed and assembled it himself. Undercarriage, wheels, tires, and bodywork: he had adapted everything to the needs in the desert. The vehicle was full of plan B's, to be ready for all eventualities or dangers. Its equipment encompassed everything that might be needed to repair, to salvage, to excavate, to tow, to transport, to groom, to nourish, to defend, to find the way, and to ram. From a night vision telescope to a refrigerator and from a TV to a microwave oven and a defibrillator, everything was at his disposal. In terms of energy, except for the fuel for the engine, the truck was completely self-sufficient, for the cabin roof and the upper part of the cistern were equipped with solar panels.

"It took me months to familiarize myself with all those gadgets. Waterman proved himself to be surprisingly patient during his explanations, demonstrations, and corrections. I was something like his sorcerer's apprentice, he used to say. As for myself, I felt rather like Ali Baba in the robbers' cave, only that I had to apply a special "Open Sesame" for every section of the unusual treasure.

"During this apprenticeship of mine, while we were driving crisscross through the desert with the truck, we shifted material of all sorts by the tons, and water in large quantities. We took turns at the wheel. While driving along, we constantly played with emergencies in our minds, for we were eager to develop plan B's not only in theory.

"Waterman avoided settled areas with his truck. If for some reason he had to visit one, he parked between the dunes, left me behind as a guard, and covered the last few kilometers with a small caterpillar, which was agile and quick like a desert fox.

"We lived like that for more than a year. Again and again, we helped tourists who found themselves in difficulties, because they thought themselves to be conquerors, explorers, or Bedouins. We led some women in high heeled shoes and miniskirts, who had ventured too far into the void, back to the green zone, here and there we repaired a broken down vehicle that wasn't roadworthy, and we provided water for people whose parched tongues hung down to their chins.

"One day, as we were taking a break to relieve ourselves southeast of the *Aïr*, we detected a dust cloud that was fast approaching from the distance. 'Plan B,' Waterman ordered anxiously, and I quickly disappeared in the metal box he had constructed between the chassis under the cistern for such emergencies. I closed the lid and could only watch what was going on through a narrow hatch.

"Waterman stood waiting . . . motionless.

"Soon, I heard the engines of two vehicles approaching, roaring, revving up and then slowing down and being cut off.

"'*Assalamu Alaykum,*' Waterman said and lifted his hand in greeting.

"The new arrivals didn't answer. Their silence did not bode well. Then I heard a few steps. One of the strangers stepped into my field of vision. I narrowly managed to suppress a cry of horror.

"The man was one of those *al-Qaida* or *ISIS* types who create hell in the desert as if it wasn't glowing hot enough already. I knew those shady types only too well, and how they turn the holy fire into an inferno. Because they were mostly clad in black and always played with fire, we called them the "charcoal burners."

"The jihadist was carrying a Kalashnikov over his shoulder. He walked around Waterman and assessed him from all sides.

"'Look here, an *ikufar*,' he said in Arabic.

"Waterman didn't bat an eyelid. He seemed to have stiffened to a salt pillar. Then I heard steps all around me. The holy warriors seemed to inspect the truck from all sides.

"Since the situation didn't bode well, I loosened the revolver from the side wall of my compartment to be ready to act, if necessary, even though my chances of survival were as unlikely as a flash flood in the *Ténéré*.

"'What are you carrying in your cistern?' asked the bearded leader with the black turban.

"'Water,' said Waterman with a hollow voice in broken Arabic. 'If you need some you can fill up your containers,' he added.

"'Then let's have a look,' said another voice, who didn't believe him.

"The two thugs disappeared from my field of vision. I heard some metallic noises and eventually the bubbling of water.

"'Water, indeed,' said the same voice as before, and the surprise could be heard. 'By Allah, what are you doing in the desert with this cistern full of water?' the holy warrior asked.

"'I take water to places that haven't got any.'

"'And where would that be?'

"'Everywhere in the desert,' said Waterman.

"I heard a dull thump and a cry of pain. Something seemed to drop down.

"'You want to make fools of us?' cried an angry voice. 'Nobody drives through the desert with a lake full of water just for fun.'

"Another dull thumping noise, probably from a foot. Then more kicks. Suddenly I saw Waterman crawling backwards. One of his eyes was blue and swollen and his lips were bleeding. The jihadist followed him and kicked him in his side again and again.

"'Come on, who are you working for and where are you taking the water?'

"'I save people who have lost their way in the desert. Look at the marks on my driver's door. Each mark stands for a life saved. I have even saved men from your ranks who were dying of thirst.'

"'Really?' asked the holy warrior. 'And you want me to believe that?'

"Then a different voice could be heard who told the leader that a certain Ahmed from another fighting brigade had told him that an *ikufar* with a cistern truck had saved his life in the middle of the desert as he had almost been dying under the scorching sun. He had told him about the marks on the door, too. The stranger might be telling the truth.

"When I heard this, I was beginning to hope again.

"The leader reflected.

"'Do you save every man you encounter?' he then asked.

"'Everyone.'

"'Soldiers, too?'

"'Everyone.'

"It wouldn't have done to lie.

"'By that, you support Allah's enemies!' decided the bearded villain and kicked Waterman again, who fell and landed on his back. Then he pointed his Kalashnikov at him.

"'I should really send a bullet through your head. But since you seem to have saved one of our people from dying, I will be lenient and let you live.'

"I hardly trusted my ears. Such a thing was very unusual with those men.

"'But we'll confiscate the truck,' said the bearded one. 'In this way, you will contribute to the *jihad*.'

"'And what about me?' asked Waterman.

"'That lies in Allah's hands.'

"So that was it! They wanted him to perish in the desert like an animal. It was worse than a bullet.

"The bearded thug turned to his companions and gave some short orders. Then I heard how the door of the truck was slammed and the engine was started. The other two vehicles sprang to life as well. Waterman had picked himself up to his knees and watched in disbelief how the convoy was about to drive off. He looked in my direction and with his lips formed a word and a letter which I guessed at once: 'Plan B!'

"But it wouldn't have been necessary. Already I held the remote control in my hands and waited for the two smaller vehicles to drive ahead. Then I pressed the right button and activated a mechanism which, if it worked as it should, released a metal box from the back of the truck that contained a survival kit and was supposed to drop in the sand. I couldn't do more at the moment. In the container there were a backpack with a full flask, a few energy bars, a thermofoil, sunglasses, a piece of string, a first aid kit, a lighter, a head lamp, a knife, a compass, a signaling mirror, and a face cloth. I had studied the plans B-one to B-thirteen very carefully.

"I was hoping the mechanism had functioned all right. If Waterman followed the advice I had given him for survival in the open desert, he could live on for three days with the survival kit in the backpack. Until then I had to find a solution to help him.

"But for the time being I was stuck in the whale belly like Yunus. Luckily, only Allah knew that I was hidden there. This was my strategic advantage.

"Thanks to the hatch I wasn't completely blind; so, I could observe that we were leaving the *Serir* and beginning to drive through a hilly area. The trip took several hours, during which I sometimes fell asleep for short periods.

"At sunset, at last, we stopped. Through the hatch I could detect hardly more than a few dry bushes. Judging from the noises, I assumed the jihadists were getting ready for the night at a certain distance from the truck. Before it was night and the jihadists had fallen asleep there was nothing I could do. So, I prepared myself to wait patiently and killed the time by trying to imagine what Waterman was doing at this moment. Had he decided to stay put at the same spot so that he could be found again more easily? But a pebbly desert wasn't the best place for survival in the heat. And he could hardly hope for a quick rescue. Was he heading towards the *Aïr*, where he could find shade or water more easily? Or was he walking in the direction of our *duar*, hoping to meet a search party from our clan at some point? Then I considered what I could do to get rid of the jihadists, and rush to the rescue of my friend. It didn't take me long to invent a plan. As soon as the jihadists were asleep, I would creep out of my hiding and would probably have to incapacitate one of their guards. The rest promised to be child's play.

"When there was no more movement and the distant voices had died down, I shifted the lid of the compartment and carefully climbed out. Luckily, the side of the truck where I cowered was situated in the shade of the young moon. When I had made sure that there was no movement among the holy warriors, I ventured to the front of the truck and peeped around the corner. In a hollow about thirty meters away, surrounded by low dry bushes, there was a dim glimmer from a few dying logs. Around the fading campfire I could guess the outlines of the sleeping men in their blankets. Close by, there stood the two command vehicles, parked near the cistern truck. No movement. But I had to stay vigilant. There was certainly a guard on duty somewhere. I peered hard in all directions, to find out where he might be posted. At last, I saw the flare of a cigarette lighter behind the second four-wheel-drive. So that's where he was. I waited some more in order to ascertain that there was no second guard, but that did not seem to be the case. The commando apparently believed they were safe enough in this remote spot.

"Without any further hesitation I loosened a pickaxe from its bracket on the side of the truck and sneaked behind the guard. He was leaning against the hood of one of their vehicles, his back turned to me. With all my force I struck the tool flat on the man's head. He collapsed without a sound. Then I remained quiet for another moment and listened hard. No movement near the campfire. I bent over the unconscious guard on the ground, took his rifle and checked his belt. To my satisfaction, I found a hunting knife, which I took. On the ground next to the man there was also a flashlight, with which I looked inside the two four-wheel-drive vehicles. There was no key in the ignition. Now I was only hoping that the driver of the cistern truck had been unable to shut off the special safety device behind the steering wheel which allowed the key to be extracted. Another plan B from Waterman inspired by Allah! I carefully opened the truck's cabin door and peered inside. Indeed, the ignition key stuck in its lock.

"The following procedure was obvious. I slit the tires of the four-wheel-drive vehicles with the hunting knife, to prevent pursuit, crept back to the truck, sat down behind the wheel, took a deep breath, started the engine, and drove off. As I was roaring past the hollow, I saw several shadows jumping and running about, then I was gone. When I heard the first shots behind me the night had already swallowed me.

"I would have preferred to return to the spot where Waterman had stayed behind, but the remaining fuel wouldn't have been enough—even with the reserve cans full—to return to our *duar*, especially if the search for him took longer. Besides, it would be more effective to search for the lonely wanderer in a group fanning out on camels.

"I took my bearing from the stars, had the accuracy of my findings confirmed by the modern instruments on board and drove back to the *duar*, which I reached at the hour of the *tazer-rahat*, the first hour of the afternoon, on the following day. On my way back, I stopped once to make sure the container with the survival kit had really come off its bracket, which luckily was the case.

"The members of the clan were astonished to see me return alone. I quickly explained to them what had happened and asked for volunteers to search for Waterman. Without exception all the men held up their hands. I selected eight of the best riders. After getting ready we waited for *l'azellewaz*, the last hour of the afternoon, so as not to burn under the afternoon sun. Then we rode off, taking an additional camel for Waterman with us. The general direction was clear. I knew I would easily find the place again where I had left him behind."

Meddur emptied his cup.

"Deprived of the modern instruments of the truck and until nightfall without orientation from the stars?" I asked in astonishment. "Did you at least have a compass?"

"Fiddlesticks! Compasses are for Europeans, because they always rush from one place to another and run the risk to lose themselves. A Targi never loses his bearings, the desert turns around him."

I could hardly imagine what he meant with this, but since the nomads seemed to have this concept in their blood, its effectiveness had most probably been tested.

Meddur again fiddled with the teapot, poured some tea, and then continued with his narrative.

"We found the spot in the morning of the following day. However, there wasn't anybody around for miles. Naturally, in accordance with his born restlessness, *ad-dalw* couldn't have chosen to sit in the pebbly desert and just wait for rescue which might never come. There were only twenty four hours left for us to find him alive, provided he had followed my instructions. But where to look for him?

"He most certainly hadn't wandered east, for that's where the desert of deserts laid. Remaining as the most likely options were the northwest, where the *Aïr* laid, the southwest, whence we had come, and possibly the south, which was closer to inhabited areas than the north.

"First, we rode in ever widening circles around the initial spot in case some trace might be discovered despite the growing wind and the pebbly ground. If we found nothing, we would split up into three groups and extend our search in a radial pattern, so as not to lose too much time. Even if we fanned out there was still the danger of missing him, but that couldn't be avoided.

"After spending the space of the fresh morning riding in circles, one of the riders found the empty container in which the survival kit had been kept. Having taken three walkie talkies from the truck with us, I was informed at once. I implored the finder not to touch or move anything. When we had reached the spot, I carefully inspected the position of the container. It didn't just lie there as if it had been thrown down carelessly, but it lay on its longer, narrower side, as if it wanted to indicate a certain direction. When I bent down, I detected on its top side an arrow of pebbles pointing northwest, in the direction of the *Aïr*. Unfortunately, we couldn't continue our search straightaway because we had reached *l'agedelsit tekkuset*, the space of the hot morning, and we first had to seek protection from the sun. But since we knew the direction in which to seek, I didn't worry too much. Waterman might possibly have to spend another night in the open desert, but this wasn't too bad, for he had the thermofoil after all. We dismounted from our camels, pitched our protective tents, and slept through the hottest part of the day.

"As *l'azellewaz*, the last hour of the afternoon, was approaching, we set off again. The direction was clear, we had to aim for the promontory of the *Aïr*. Silently, we rode through the evening and the night to reduce the distance to Waterman.

"Shortly after our break for our morning prayers, we saw the shape of the *Aïr* rising from the shimmering ground in the distance. My main worry was that we could have missed or overtaken the wanderer during the night. I guessed the number of hours of his walk, the approximate distance he might have covered, compared the result with the hours and the distance of our own trip and concluded that we would get to him before reaching the *Aïr*. Unless he had changed his direction or been prevented from continuing his walk for some reason and lay somewhere behind us. To increase our chances, we split up again. One *mehari* continued in the direction of the *Aïr*, another one rode back the way we had come, and the rest swarmed out on both sides of our path in order to cover more of the wide terrain.

"We rode for hours through the desert without success. I began to worry a little, for we ought to have found the missing man hours before. During the hottest time around *la tarrut* we had to interrupt our search again and resumed it in the late afternoon.

"Suddenly there was a crackle in my walkie-talkie. One of our riders in the south had found a heap of rocks, a small stone pyramid. Was that a sign left by Waterman? I told the others to keep searching where they were and rode to where the cairn had been found. When I arrived there in the setting sun I determined that the stones had no doubt been heaped up by a human hand. Most probably it was the work of Waterman. It seemed that he had come away from his original route, for the mark lay outside the direction we had taken. In the hope of finding another cairn we surrounded the *rukam min hijara* in ever widening circles. Just before sunset we found another stone heap, so now we knew the direction taken by Waterman with the help of his compass.

"We slowly rode through the night, which was dimly illuminated by moon and stars, but it was enough for our fanned out group to detect eventual marks and signs. We found four or five more cairns, but then the pebbles gave way to sand, in which the wind had covered up all possible tracks. Gradually, our environment was changing into a dune landscape, which rendered our task considerably more difficult. Still, we rode on, keeping the same direction. After the sun had long risen, we stopped on the crest of a tall star shaped dune. All around us, the glowing golden sand of the dunes rose to heaven. I fetched Waterman's binoculars from the saddlebag and searched the surroundings. Nothing.

"'What the desert wants to keep belongs to it,' I anxiously reflected. Also, a man lost in the desert is already a dead man in his head long before his body gives up, because he has no objective, no aim. The desert is like life: immoderate. And this immoderation paralyzes one's survival drive because it opposes every concrete objective.

"As I was about to lower my binoculars, I suddenly saw a quick flash and looked again more carefully. There! Again! Something seemed to sway in the morning breeze, reflecting the light. We got on our camels and rode towards whatever it was that flashed up at regular intervals. When we came nearer, we discovered a camel's rib bone stuck in the sand on top of a dune, from which hung a hand mirror at the end of a string. But where was Waterman?

"As soon as we could see over the top of the dune, we detected a kind of emergency shelter in the hollow behind, from which a pair of feet in mountain boots stuck out. We descended and approached the man who was lying outstretched under the shelter and partly dug in. He was unconscious, his breath was weak, and his heartbeat was irregular, but he was alive! We immediately infused him with some water, but not too much, and we pitched one of our tents, in whose shade we laid him down. While some of us were busy setting up camp to stay through the hottest time of the day, I cooled the survivor's face and lips with a moistened cloth. Then I inspected his shielding device. What had allowed him to stabilize the thermofoil as an emergency shelter was a camel's ribcage sticking out of the sand, next to which some human bones were scattered about. The whole time, he had lain in the belly of a dead *mehari*, whose bones stood around him like thin pillars. Yunus in a dry fish!

"I went pale with awe. Allah had indeed made use of death to keep my friend alive. '*La hauwla wa la Quwwata illa billah*, there is no force nor power except from Allah,' I murmured.

"Hours later, Waterman slowly came to his senses. When, after several relapses into unconsciousness, he recognized me at last, a smile appeared on his lips.

"'Look here, my plan B,' he breathed and went back to sleep.

"We had to wait for two days until our friend seemed able to stay in a saddle. Then we tied him as best we could onto the camel that we had brought with us for that purpose and rode back to the *duar*.

"My friend really had a remarkable *baraka*.

"As we were swaying on the backs of our *meharis* I called to him over my shoulder that this time his life had been saved by the bones of the past, and not by modern technology.

"'You are forgetting the thermofoil.'

"'A simple cotton shawl would have done the same trick.'

"He didn't reply for a while.

"Then he uttered the strangest sentence I had ever heard from him:

"'At some point, I will be killed by life, not by death.'

"Although I thought of those mysterious words for a long time, I couldn't find the key to their meaning."

Due to his increasing tiredness, Meddur's voice eventually dried to a murmur, and I had to make an effort to grasp his last words before he fell asleep. His sentences were losing their coherence. He seemed to be soaring on the brink of dreams.

"The stars," he murmured, "their light in me . . . the inner compass . . . everything is better than plan B. Bones to the bones . . . and shade is life . . . also the shadow of death. Death protects against death . . . I must become a corpse in order to survive."

Then, only the sleeper's regular breathing could be heard.

I checked my watch: four o'clock in the morning.

Time to lie down for a few hours as well, although I felt more awake than ever, because what I'd heard was hauntingly lingering in my head.

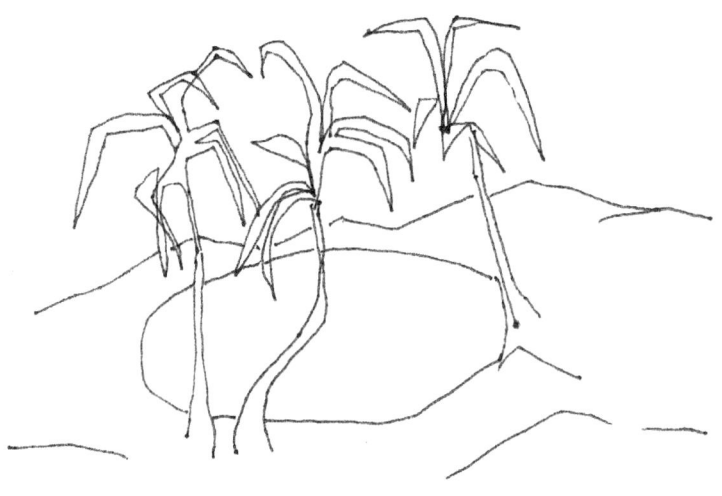

Third Day

I missed Meddur's prayers on the following day.
When I opened my eyes, the sun was already high up in the sky. The Targi seemed to be waiting for my awakening to boil tea.

Hardly had he seen that I'd opened my eyes when he started the gas cooker. I fetched some biscuits, dried fruit, nuts, and a box of Lokum from the Land Rover.

We made ourselves comfortable, sipped our tea with pleasure, nibbled and chewed our food.

Without preamble, Meddur began to talk of Waterman again.

"A story has only reached its end when it has come full circle," he said. "And what concerns Waterman's story, it hasn't come full circle by a long shot yet. It might have been if he hadn't been the man he was. But he was a restless, driven soul. Like the camel, he belonged to the cold sphere, which made the warm sphere desirable yet unattainable for him. While he was converting us from nomads to resident settlers, he himself, who came from the world of the residents, gradually became an errant knight. But in contrast to the real nomads, the desert through which he roamed was actually inside him. He seemed a stranger to himself and to the outside world.

"That was never more evident than when he undressed to wash himself. His pale skin appeared to me like a white, old fashioned bathing suit from a soap commercial, from which were sticking out only the tanned arms and the ruddy neck with the head on top as real parts of the body. His nakedness clothed him.

His blue eyes were utterly unfit for the desert; that's why he never went outside without his sunglasses. Then there were the tics which seized him when he had to sit still somewhere. Then his face muscles began to twitch, and his right leg shook and trembled so that it was a pity. He appeared like a flapping fish caught by an evil fisherman.

"No doubt, he was possessed by the *djinn* of restlessness, by some fidgeting demon. He moved all the time, to escape from the death in his heart. His journey was not one of discovery, but a flight. Like a spiky round bush blown about by the wind, he was driven hither and thither by inner squalls, and he scratched everything on his way.

"Sometimes he seemed to me like one of those traveling stones, whose only aim it is to leave deep ruts in the ground. I wondered how such a death defying man could be so lifesaving.

"Having learned to like him and having received, little by little, some modest signs of esteem from him, I asked him if he had ever considered sharing his life with a woman. He didn't even engage in the topic and suddenly had some important problem to solve under the hood of his truck."

For a while, Meddur was lost in thought. When he looked at me again, he had a strange radiance in his eyes.

"In the desert, a man without a woman is a lonely rider who is exposed to the demons. It is only in a woman's tent where he can find protection from the evil spirits that haunt him all around. That was what Waterman lacked."

Then he asked: "What do you think? Why do only women play the *imzad*?"

I shrugged my shoulders, having no clue.

"Because the *imzad* contains the essence of femininity. That's why we men dance and invent poems to its sound again and again. That is our answer to the call of the feminine. It's how the vital balance between men and women develops in the desert. The *imzad* is a good spirit that attracts other good spirits. Its horsehair string creates an equilibrium by its vibrations. If you can't hear the *imzad*, you ignore the rules and regulations. And if you ignore the rules and regulations of the desert, you will be devoured by the jackal. The *imzad* is a mystery like a woman, a mystery that knows and expresses everything. It can only be understood by the heart. That's something that the Arabs have never understood. They keep their women like chickens and are therefore condemned to puff themselves up like cockerels. In contrast, the *imohar* consider a woman as a fountain around which the men gather. She gives life, like water. She is the triangle which is the motif on the saddlecloths that we always carry with us. While we are riding around on our camels, the symbol of the seated woman and her tent safeguards our balance. We may be restless, eternal travelers in the infinity of the desert, but within this infinity we have a firm base to which we will always return. As the mistress of the tent, woman constitutes this base. Woman and tent are one. When we enter a woman's home, we enter the realm of the feminine. Only a woman's tent can protect us against the width of the space that we roam. Even more: By bearing children the women renew time."

In the ensuing silence I inserted the timid question: "What did Waterman have to do with all of this?"

"Waterman? Well . . . " Meddur scratched his head. "How to express this? . . . His impatience and his inner unrest were not ideal conditions to envisage the long courting ritual which might have led to success with one of our women. Still, I didn't give up the idea of finding a female companion for him, for he lacked the equilibrium of the triangle, the balance, the protection of the tent.

"One day, chance came to my assistance.

"Among our clan there lived a widow whose husband had passed away from a long illness some years ago. Her name was Kahina, and she had a daughter of nine years, Lunja, with whom she looked after our goat herd. Concerning the goats and the female goat keepers, you have to know . . . "

Again, Meddur's thoughts had flown off and lost themselves in another wide digression about female goat keepers and their animals. I didn't even try to stop him and to lead him back to the path of his narrative. For, on one hand I had as much time as a desert bird has feathers, and on the other hand I found his comments on the peculiarities of nomadic life most instructive.

He explained to me that, contrary to appearances, looking after goats was a very hard job and required a great deal of empathy, sensitivity, and above all a favorable star. Without common sense, brains, and a good portion of intuition, one couldn't make a success of it. Female goat keepers had to be willing to work hard and be able to go without sleep for a long time, for the milking of the goats usually began in the early morning. Then the animals grazed for ten hours, during which time it was not uncommon for a herd to cover some forty kilometers in search of grass.

The goats were vital for the nomads because the camels didn't give birth often enough to provide sufficient milk for regular nourishment. Moreover, the milk of camels wasn't ideal for cheese-making, while cheese—and milk—formed the most important basic nutriment of the Tuareg. He added that goats used to be something like money on four legs, *éhéré*.

Finally, Meddur, in accordance with his character, became philosophical again.

"The herd," he said, "flows like water. The same as when you catch water, there is no vacant time, otherwise the goats will lose themselves in the desert like water that seeps away in the sand. The herdswoman isn't an alien element stamped on by some exterior force to watch over the herd, no, she is part of the herd, as she is part of the pasture, of the water, of thirst and hunger. Like every nomad, she carefully economizes with the little she has.

"Herdswomen are Abel's daughters. They move in a space in which nothing is stable. But they are not governed by things. For their freedom is a precondition for the keeping of the immutable, unwritten laws, it requires the keeping of a balance between humans, animals, and vegetation, so that water can become milk. Only like this, the desert can turn into a garden."

I helplessly scratched my head. The void around me certainly didn't bear any resemblance to a garden.

Then the Targi's features cleared up and his words entered areas of mysticism.

"Herdswomen are magicians," he said. "They have arisen directly from the source of life itself, and they know neither marks nor limitations. They are pure movement, guardians of order in a space which is interior and exterior at the same time. By their magic power, they withstand the pull of this space, which is open in all directions. This in contrast to the sons of Cain, who are confined in their cultures because they try to set limits to space and to stop the flow of time. Believe me: God has never sent a prophet who was not a herdsman.

"The herdswoman has an acute ear for what goes on in the herd. Frequently and with pleasure she speaks with her favorite goat. Since she has given every goat a name, the animals will trot up to her when they are called. At night, they gather around her tent and need not be looked after like other domestic animals.

"Our herdswomen's enemy is the *kumbultu*, the jackal, which they imagine like a werewolf. It constantly attempts to spread death and bring chaos into the flock. It is the unrestrained wild element, the cruel fate which may strike everywhere and at all times and can only be conjured up by knowledge of the secretion."

"The secretion?"

"The secretion lies in the flow of water, of blood, of milk and of sperm. The secretion is movement. It is life itself."

I nodded my head even though I didn't really understand what obviously lay beyond cognitive understanding.

The Targi seemed to want to test my patience, for instead of directing his discourse at last to Waterman and his difficult relationship with women, he appeared to prolong his fumbling with the teapot on purpose. Only when the beverage was finally bubbling in the cups did he take up the trail of his narrative again.

"Well then, one day the herdswoman I mentioned, Kahina, came to me and asked me—since I was *ad-dalw's* closest confidant and the clan's *Amghar*—how she should best behave towards the stranger, because she was quite fond of him. Unfortunately, he didn't appear to react to her discreet signals. On the other hand, she constantly felt his eyes on her. That was puzzling.

"Having observed the flirtations between those two from the distance for quite a while, her words didn't surprise me. It was no wonder that Waterman was attracted by the full forms, the thick long hair, and the shining, white teeth of the woman. Many a man in the clan had attempted to conquer her tent before him. But so far, the dark beauty had rejected every candidate. It was odd that she should now melt in the face of this restless, introverted stranger.

"'Invite him to dinner,' I suggested. 'Otherwise, you may have to wait forever.'

"'If he's really so shy, he'll reject the invitation and crawl back into his hole like a gerbil,' she answered.

"No doubt women are the better experts on masculine psychology, I sighed to myself. She was right. A frontal attack could only lead to failure. So, I offered Kahina to accept the role of go between and present Waterman as gently as possible with her invitation.

"Soon, I invited Waterman to tea in my tent and began to explain to him the advantages of female companionship by referring to my own wife, who was busy around the tent and supported my words by smiling at him.

"He waved off.

"'That's nothing for me. I have been through the whole exercise before and I haven't made a positive experience.'

"'You were married?'

"'Unfortunately, yes. It lasted a few years and ended in divorce. I even have a son somewhere in Europe. I last saw him when he was about eight. Out of distress, I left my home and started to work in Libya as an engineer in the oil drilling industry.'

"'I see. That's what you meant with building pyramids when we first met?'

"He nodded.

"I had landed in a *cul de sac* with my mediation project, but I didn't want to let go of the gazelle of my intention. So, I cleverly argued that there was also a plan B in one's love life, which amounted to a second chance.

"He had to smile at my curious application of his favorite argument. Then he grew serious again and repaid my argument in the same currency: 'As you keep saying, I am carrying a wide desert and the djinn of unrest in me. But when you live in a tent you need trust and serenity, otherwise there will soon be a worse sandstorm in the matrimonial space than outside between the dunes. Am I right?'

"Unfortunately, he was.

"Not knowing how to go on, I poured some more tea and offered him some more biscuits. Then I cautiously steered the conversation to other matters.

"Shortly before he left my tent, I casually mentioned that I was invited to dinner at Kahina's that night and asked him if he wanted to come with me. You should have seen his gaze, Jean. I had never seen such a wispy stare before. He seemed to be torn apart and stood petrified before me.

"Then he looked straight into my eyes.

"'Have you asked her if I could come with you?'

"'We are both invited.'

"'I see.'

"He hesitated for a moment, then to my astonishment he said: 'Okay,' turned round and disappeared.

"I dried the sweat that stood on my brow from the strain and sat down to calm down my cramped stomach with a nice cup of tea. The discussion with him hadn't gone as expected, but what counted after all was the result. When I had recovered, I let Kahina know through one of my children that the stranger would attend her dinner."

Meddur again fumbled with the teapot.

"And?" I asked impatiently. "Did he really come?"

Meddur took his time to answer.

"Yes," he said at last, "he came."

"And?"

"There is no 'and.'"

"How come?"

"Well, at first everything went well. As I had advised Waterman, he presented the hostess with a shawl of blue silk, some sugar, and some tea.

"Then we sat down around the flat bread baked in sand with vegetable sauce and we enjoyed millet, dates, cheese, and milk. Kahina looked ravishing in her golden dress with the emerald-green belt, and she had indeed made a great effort with the preparation of the delicious meal."

"What went wrong?"

"Well, I found myself sitting between two mute and tense creatures of God who didn't dare to look at each other. So, I filled the gaping silence with my own comments and tried to bridge what couldn't be bridged over."

I could vividly imagine the situation described by the Targi. He in the middle with his overflowing gush of words, feigning a discussion between three people, taking over both missing voices, commenting on things that weren't said, building up banalities into meaningful arguments, and capitulating in the end.

"So your attempt sank in the *fesh-fesh*, the quicksand."

"That's it, and in the face of such a painful defeat, I gave up my career as a matchmaker at once."

"I can understand that."

"Not to be understood, however, is the fact that, in the dusk of the following evening, I saw Kahina step up to Waterman, take his hand in hers and make some mysterious signs with her finger, signs he couldn't possibly understand. Even more incomprehensible is the fact that he let her do it!"

"What sort of signs were they?"

"In our culture, that's the way women give men to understand how they want to make love with them."

"And what did Waterman do?"

"He allowed Kahina to lead him by his hand and to my great astonishment disappeared with her in her tent, from where he only emerged again on the following morning."

"Bless my soul! And how did he justify his change of mood afterwards?"

"We did not mention it. However, I couldn't resist to draw his attention to the fact that sometimes plan B can be more agreeable than plan A. He pretended to not hear the remark, and in the time to come he gave in to plan B in Kahina's tent for many nights."

In silence we sipped our tea and ruminated over the numerous imponderables of love.

Then Meddur's voice could be heard with a sorrowful undertone.

"Unfortunately, the moments of happiness on this earth are as fleeting as the blossoms of the acacia in spring. Several weeks after that strange conversion of Waterman's the heat of the sun threw black shadows on our *duar*. The jihadists hadn't forgotten the trick I had played on them. They had been looking for me for months and were now near their objective.

"Fortunately, one of our hunters saw them approaching out there in the plain, jumped on his camel and raised the alarm.

"What should we do? From our tracks they would find us within hours, even though our oasis was situated in a hollow and partly sheltered by the surrounding *gam*.

"Should we leave everything as it was and hide in the hills? Many of us favored this.

"If it really was the group whose tires I had slit open, we would have a problem. They would recognize the cistern truck and want to know how it had come here. Jihadists have no mercy. They don't negotiate. They kill everything that's in their way.

"Could the truck be driven somewhere else in time, somewhere it couldn't be seen? But where? In the only passable direction, the jihadists were driving around with their pick- ups. And there would be tracks that couldn't be wiped out so easily.

"At last, the tribe decided to take flight, for property could always be replaced, but not lost life. So, the whole tribe disappeared behind the hillcrest. I remained and sat down in the sand, my back to the tents.

"Waterman asked me what that was for.

"'I am staying here, and I will try to tell them some more or less credible story. Am I not a story-teller?'

"'They will kill you, no matter if they believe your story or not.'

"'That is only for Allah to decide. Perhaps I can persuade them by negotiation not to destroy everything here. You wouldn't want all that you have built up over months razed to the ground, would you?'

"'No. That's why we need a plan B.'

"I waved off, surrendering to fate. 'Do what you have to do. I'm staying here.'

"'You with your improvisations . . .'

"Waterman shook his head at my stubbornness and disappeared.

"After about an hour, an off-road vehicle appeared, occupied by four black clad holy warriors, and stopped.

"One of them checked our *seribas*, *gourbis* and tents with his binoculars. When he couldn't discern any movement, he turned his binoculars in my direction and observed me carefully.

"Then the vehicle started again and approached to a few meters from me. Three of the jihadists jumped down and secured their position with raised Kalashnikovs. The fourth, apparently their leader, took his time getting off. Then he looked at me. We were in *l'agedelsit semmidet*, the space of the fresh morning, the sun was still low in the sky. The black bearded leader with deep set, coal black eyes approached me without drawing the revolver which he was carrying at his belt.

"He raised his hand in greeting and tried to appear friendly.

"'*Assalamu Alaykum*,' he said.

"'*Assalam*.'

"'*Fi amanillah*—may Allah protect you,' he added.

"'*Hayyāka Allāh wa Bayyāk*—may Allah greet you and prepare your place in Paradise. Be my guest. My tent and my possessions are yours.'

"He nodded his head, sat down in the sand opposite me and scrutinized me with his piercing eyes.

"'I thank you for your hospitality', he said, 'but I regret that the members of your clan have not stayed behind to welcome us. Such distrust hurts me.'

"'In times that are unsafe, Allah recommends precaution to the defenseless', I invented a proverb by way of reply.

"'May I offer you some tea?' I asked then, following our tradition.

"He waved off with a blunt gesture.

"'Let's not play games', he said. 'I haven't come to have tea with a camel driver. I'm interested in the truck behind you.'

"I didn't turn round, as if the object was of no interest.

"'Oh, that? Some foreigner left it here in payment for a camel a few months ago. He was going to come back some time to recuperate it, but he hasn't returned yet.'

"'Don't try to fool me.'

"'*Bi idhnillah*, with Allah's permission, I insist on what I said.'

"'And why are your people in hiding like gerbils?'

"'As I said, not all visitors are as peaceful as you.'

"'In the name of Allah, the gracious and merciful, you are right, I am a peaceful man, as long as I'm not lied to. And you are lying. You and your people stole this truck from us a few months ago and slit the tires of my men's vehicles. Unfortunately, two of our ten warriors died on their long walk back to base camp. Those dead men are crying for revenge.'

"With these words, he pulled out his revolver from its holster and carelessly pointed it at my head.

"'Well, my friend, you will now order your people to come back here and surrender the *ikufar* who owns this truck and who is probably still hiding among your people. Otherwise...'

"The movement he made with his gun was unmistakable.

"It appeared that I wasn't a good enough storyteller to fool a jihadist.

"'With your behavior you are violating the holy laws of hospitality twice', I said in desperation and closed my eyes in expectation of his bullet. In my anguish, a last, helpless argument came to my mind. 'Before pulling the trigger, consider that my people and I ride exclusively on camels and have no idea of motor vehicles.'

"The jihadist was not convinced by this and only repeated his threat with a dangerous undertone in his voice: 'Call your people, or I will fetch them myself.'

"'They won't come, and you won't find them,' I replied. 'And what concerns my life, it is in Allah's hands, not in yours. *Audhu-billah*, I seek refuge with Allah.'

"He looked at me as if he was dealing with a madman. Nothing could save me now. I closed my eyes a second time.

"However, to my surprise, Allah had another plan B in store for me than death.

"When no bullet came and I looked at life again I saw how my tormentor's three companions were backing away to their vehicle, swaying their guns. The bearded leader's eyes flashed up with uncertainty. Slowly, he stood up from the ground and began to walk backwards in the direction of his men. It was as if he had seen a ghost.

"My jaw dropped in astonishment.

"A doomed man just a moment ago, my life resumed some color with every step of the jihadists' retreat. At last, the holy warriors jumped in their vehicle, drove round a sharp bend, and disappeared with howling engine.

"Perplexed, I turned round.

"What I saw nearly took my breath away. Behind every palm tree, every tent and *seriba* there peeped half a Targi armed with an automatic gun. No wonder the jihadists had lost their courage in the face of such superior power. I shook my head and looked for Waterman. As he didn't seem to be around, I entered the *duar* and found him kneeling behind a tent where he followed the jihadists through the viewfinder of a bazooka. When they had been swallowed up by the desert he stood up with a smile on his lips.

"'That did the trick,' he said laconically.

"'That was probably your plan B? Why didn't you tell me you had a store of guns?'

"'First, the guns were plan A, for your stubborn suicide strategy doesn't deserve the label "plan" by any stretch of the imagination. Secondly, I'm afraid I have no ammunition for these guns. And thirdly, I had a plan B anyway, because for this bazooka I do have a few grenades. Any more questions?'

"I could hardly believe it. I had been saved by a bluff which wasn't really a bluff.

"'*Shukran*—thank you,' I said with a trembling voice. 'But they are sure to come back with heavy enforcement.'

"'Maybe, but this time we have the time to rehearse a whole range of plans, haven't we?'

"That might very well have been. But I didn't see how we could win against a whole bunch of heavily armed terrorists without rifle ammunition and with only one bazooka."

Meddur interrupted his narrative and clumsily stood up to urinate.

"All that tea . . . " he said.

I went in the opposite direction and did the same.

Soon we were sitting under the benevolent umbrella of the acacia again, which formed a nearly round island of shade in the shimmering heat. The sun was approaching its zenith, and it seemed to be planning to bake the surface of the *Ténéré* like a pancake. Nothing was stirring under the glowing sun. No breath of air was moving the leaves of the acacia, no insect was buzzing through the air. In addition, there reigned the leaden silence which made us feel our heartbeats like deafening gong strokes. Our eyes skimmed the deadly plain.

"The sun burns the careless like Allah's word burns the ignoramus," said Meddur suddenly out of the blue.

"What do you mean?"

"The fanatic holy warriors are like dogs chained to the *Holy Qur'an*, which they can hardly read. Invisible leads hold them prisoners. They want to compress their whole lives, nay the whole world into the holy written signs until things become so rigid and narrow that they freeze. But they have an additional problem with the desert. If a man tries to compress the desert into narrow notions, he doesn't create width but void, because the eternity of the godly spirit is caught up by time and runs out like sand in an hourglass. That's why I distrust the written signs. They can so easily be separated from the spirit that inhabits them. Symbols tend to make themselves independent from humans and then serve death instead of life. As soon as the suffering of the poor creature no longer fills the symbols with humanity, and humans let themselves be governed by them, they become strangers to themselves.

"Muhammad—may Allah's blessing and peace be upon him—once said: 'Wisdom is a dot. Only ignorance expands it.' *Bismillahi r-rahmani r-rahimi*—in the name of Allah, the gracious and merciful—the *Holy Qur'an*, nay the entire universe, is contained in the dot of the letter *bâ* (ب) in the *Basmala*, which is the first Sura at the beginning of our holy scripture. Everything has flown from it, and everything flows back to it. It is this dot that really matters. Everything can spring from it: hatred or love, happiness or sorrow, good and evil. It only depends on what we make of it. Do we condemn it to rigidity by trying to throw the writing which emerges from life over the reality like a net, or do we breathe life into it so that its spirit can spread its wings and move freely?

"The reduction of life to written signs kills the spirit which is contained in every object and in every human being. It paralyzes the being that has emerged from time, by a deadly timelessness. The jihad of the heart is destroyed by the jihad of materiality. In reality, the holy warriors aren't any better than the infidels that they pretend to be fighting against. Thus, their violence is directed against themselves and is in contradiction to the openness of the letter *bâ*."

Then Meddur spread out his prayer rug, knelt down and performed his midday devotions.

I admired this man's wisdom. He performed his prayers without being imprisoned by them, he obeyed the unwritten laws contained in the holy scripture, thereby remaining a free man, and he could face death without fear because he had always taken care of his soul.

After finishing his prayers, the Targi stood up again and winked at me. "Life and death can wait if necessary," he said, "but not a good story."

After I had made myself comfortable on my mat as well as it was possible in this seething heat, I was ready to listen to him.

"As soon as the jihadists had disappeared, we held a long consultation about what to do. Some of us wanted to fight and defend our *duar* to the last drop of blood. Others reminded us that, as *imohars*, we had to move around constantly to escape death. Still others thought we should pursue the holy warriors and, taking advantage of the element of surprise, destroy them. While we were discussing we forgot the time. We were careless and didn't expect the jihadists' retaliation so soon, since we thought that the group that we had chased away would need some time to get reinforcement.

"We were wrong.

"While we were still weighing the pros and cons of the arguments, Lunja came running, frightened, screaming and crying. She gasped for breath and trembled so, that we could hardly understand a word of what she was trying to tell us. She spluttered something about a 'holy fire of the jihad,' of 'divine revenge' and 'just punishment'.

"When, at last, we managed to make sense of her scraps of words and broken sentences, we looked at one another in puzzlement. Waterman went grey in his face. His stare was frightening. Without uttering a word, he went to his store shed and presently returned with a strange, heavy gun on which a telescopic sight was mounted. Over his shoulder he was carrying a bag in which loud rattle could be heard when he, who had always mounted a camel clumsily and hesitantly, now nimbly jumped on one and rode off like an experienced Targi. It seemed as if he was born on the back of a camel. After recovering from our shock, we all rushed to our animals and chased after him.

"After a seemingly endless ride, we reached the pastures in the south where the goats were grazing at this time of the year. From far off, we saw Waterman's camel nibbling at some dry bushes.

"As we were approaching the scene we were horrified.

"All over the ground lay dead goats with cut throats.

"Waterman was kneeling near the dead body of his beloved Kahina, whose head had been cut off and spiked on a wooden stick. The mad dogs who dared to call themselves holy warriors hadn't run the risk of attacking the *duar*, which seemed to be defended by heavily armed men. To give cruel emphasis to their demands they had attacked us where it would hurt us most. They had struck our livlihood, the goats, to subjugate us. We had gathered from Lunja's stammering that there would be much more bloodshed if we didn't surrender the truck and its driver.

"We stood aghast and with bowed heads at the sight of such carnage perpetrated in the name of Allah.

"Waterman cried bitterly.

"'It is my fault,' he blurted out. 'I carry death in my soul and contaminate everything that comes in touch with me.'

"I stepped up to him and laid my hand on his shoulder. 'Why am I still alive although I have been very close to you for so long? You carry no blame. Everything you do is intended to save lives.'

"At these words, I felt a spasm run through his body.

"'That can change,' he said with a cold voice, stood up and returned to his camel with firm steps.

"I understood straightaway what he had in mind, and I followed him to dissuade him from his intentions. But he wouldn't listen to me, mounted his camel, and rode off. I turned round to my companions and told them to ride back to our tent village and to hide in the mountains with the rest of our clan, for safety. Just in case, an armed reconnaissance patrol was to remain near the *duar*. This was not a very promising plan B, but I couldn't think of any better idea at the moment.

"Then I mounted my camel and rode after Waterman.

"Because he had to follow the jihadists' tracks, I managed to catch up with him soon. The warriors seemed to have taken some of the goats with them to fill their bellies with the meat, for we found several blood marks.

"During our ride, I tried to change his mind again, but I couldn't get him off his plans. I reminded him that our enemies were much stronger in numbers and entreated him to look after our clan's safety first and to attack the jihadists with a strong reinforcement later.

"He wouldn't listen to me and concentrated on the tracks of our enemies.

"Not wanting to leave him alone, I reluctantly followed him. Like this we continued for many hours. My entreaties soon petered out under the seething heat, and then even the bloody tracks on the soil ended. Luckily the ground, which had meanwhile turned into a pebbly desert, gradually became sandier, which made the tire tracks of the vehicles stand out more clearly, thus compensating us for the disappearance of the bloody traces.

"Waterman suddenly turned left and rode towards a *gam*, a foothill of the *Aïr*, which we reached after some time. At the bottom of the *gam* he dismounted, pulled out his gun from its sheath and climbed to the top of the hill. There he unfolded the gun's legs and lay down to peer through the telescopic sight.

"I got out my binoculars—a present from Waterman which I always carried with me—and I could discern a thin column of smoke in the distance. Around it, I could see the vehicles of the holy warriors, who were obviously busy roasting the meat of the stolen goats. They had to feel very safe to set up camp on the open plain, at a relatively short distance from our *duar*.

"Through the telescopic sight, Waterman scanned the group's closer surroundings.

"Then he mounted his camel again without a word and rode further along the side of the *gam* opposite the holy warriors. He apparently wanted to approach them as near as possible under cover of the hill. I stowed my binoculars in my saddlebag and rode after him. After some time, he got off his camel, climbed to the edge of the hill and again lay down with his gun. Again, he observed the camp of the holy warriors, which I judged to lie still out of the reach of his gun.

"To my surprise, he corrected the position of his body, improved the firm hold of his gun's legs, relaxed his neck and shoulders, pressed his eye to the sight and took aim carefully.

"'But you won't . . . at this distance?'

"The first shot rang out. Then others followed at regular intervals. Waterman worked like a machine, methodically, regularly, and precisely.

"I looked through my binoculars and observed the scene in the distance.

"The fierce warriors ran about like stirred up chickens, looked in all directions and blindly fired shots into the void, probably more to build up courage than to hit anything, for the well camouflaged gunman couldn't be detected and by no means reached at this distance.

"To my astonishment, not a single warrior dropped to the ground despite the numerous shots.

"Nervously I adjusted the focus of my binoculars and I soon understood why: Waterman was content to shoot the tires of the vehicles and the containers for water and fuel of the jihadists, which he achieved with admirable precision although we were more than two kilometers away from our enemies. What a gun! And what a marksman!

"After several rounds he assessed the damage done, appeared to be satisfied and quietly walked back to his camel.

"Through my binoculars, I looked at the vehicles in flames and at the black men who were desperately running about, before I followed him.

"At the bottom of the hill I resolutely planted myself before him when he was about to mount his camel again.

"What's the point? Why didn't you just shoot the dogs?"

"Just for once, let Allah provide plan B", he said dryly.

"But if . . . "

"He interrupted me impatiently: 'You explained to me in detail how one cannot survive in the desert without sticking together and keeping a balance.'

"I nodded.

"'In this case, those down there are as good as dead, for they don't know one or the other.'

"Then he pushed me aside, got on his camel and disappeared.

"Of course, he was fundamentally right. But I preferred to mistrust the evidence and stay there to keep an eye on the jihadists. One could never know. Perhaps it was Allah's intention to punish Waterman's negligence. After all, he was just an *ikufar*.

"The warriors seemed to have saved a few flasks and a water canister from the devastation. It would have been enough for a Tuareg group to reach inhabited areas. But those fighters apparently weren't Bedouins, for they started to walk away like idiots in the full heat of the sun instead of waiting for the evening in the shade of the smoke and the destroyed vehicles. Even though every stronghold in the desert is doomed to be ruined, such a ruin may offer a lifesaving shade for some time before it disappears in the sand. But every man who walks under the merciless midday sun without protection becomes a shadeless being, a being of pure light that swelters in a boiling hell. This hell hits everyone who wants to be only light and despises the shades.

"Remember this, Jean: Whoever, in his submission to light, gives absolute meaning to the writing and neglects nature, is rightfully condemned to death.

"Well, I let the gang pass and followed the warriors at a safe distance. Hours later, I found the first weapons dropped in the sand, then some empty flasks. On the following day, the first dead bodies lay around the desert. Desiccated bodies with bloated faces from which the skin was peeling off in shreds. Those who were still alive were facing the same fate. The lack of water was attacking their kidney function and poisoning them, thickening their blood. Soon, their hearts would fail.

"Allah's justice was hitting them with merciless cruelty. The blood which they had shed so carelessly was taking its revenge. In a way, they were choking in their own bloodthirsty madness.

"On the third day I heard some shots being fired.

"When the noise had trailed away, I carefully approached them with my gun at the ready, leading my camel by the reins.

"The scene that I encountered left no doubt about what had happened.

"Around the last undamaged water canister—I registered that it was still half full—were spread out the dead bodies of the last three warriors. Obviously, they had shot each other in their fight over the last remaining water. I shook my head. These pitiful men were not even able to die with dignity. They were proof of the fact that the best always brings forth the worst if we turn away from our inner laws. Then the jihad devours its own children.

"Anyway, we were safe for the time being . . . until a different gang of this type would find its way to our village.

"When I reached our still deserted *duar* a day later, I first looked for Waterman in vain. Then I saw that the door to his shed stood half open. I entered and let my eyes get used to the darkness. Then I rummaged around, knocking over some automatic rifles, and to my surprise noticed a whole big pile of boxes full of ammunition. I made sure that the ammunition was suitable for the rifles by loading one of them with a few cartridges. No doubt, they fitted. I stood there perplexed and couldn't make sense of it.

"Then I heard a whimper at the other end of the store, and I approached the sound. Soon I found Waterman, who was sitting on the ground with his back to the wall, uttering desperate sounds. Filled with consternation, I took him in my arms and pressed him to me as though I could dispel the djinn of unrest from him like this.

"When he had calmed down, I reported to him the death throes of the jihadists.

"'The desert has proved you right,' I added.

"He only nodded his head.

"Then I dared to ask the difficult question that was burning on my tongue.

"'Why didn't you give our people any ammunition for their rifles when the holy warriors first appeared, given that there is such a lot of it here?'

"He took his time to answer. He seemed to be struggling for words.

"At last, he said: 'The death of the first lot of jihadists would only have produced an escalation of violence which the *duar* wouldn't have survived. And I didn't want to burden the members of the clan with a bloody guilt.'

"'But you were ready to kill the four jihadists with your bazooka!'

"'That was only plan B in case of absolute necessity. And a plan B is only really a good plan if it doesn't need to be carried out. In any case, it is a different thing for me,' he said. So, it came that I learned his secret at last."

"What secret?"

"Years before the events which I have just told you about, he had—as I already mentioned—left his home after a painful divorce and accepted a job as an engineer on an oilfield in Libya. The location was protected because the oil company had made an agreement with a terror militia and stood under its protection. One day, while that militia was away on another fighting spree, an opposing troop of *Al-Qaida* fighters appeared at the site. Waterman was just busy looking for a spare part for a pump in the store building when he heard shots and loud voices shouting commands in the area outside. He hid in an empty wooden box and waited for the jihadists to leave after searching the store for hidden workers. Then he climbed out of his hiding, rushed upstairs, where there were kept some guns, quickly loaded one of them, as well as some reserve magazines, and crept to one of the windows. When he peered outside, he saw that the holy warriors had forced his fellow workers to kneel down in a row with their hands at the back of their necks. He should have shot his gun, but he didn't do it, until it was too late, and his companions had been mown down by a round from a Kalashnikov. Why had he hesitated? He couldn't account for it himself. From fear, perhaps, or because he just couldn't bring himself to wipe out human lives. Whatever the reason, he had hesitated too long, and now he couldn't forgive himself for this, and he couldn't forgive himself either for the fact that he had been working for an oil company for whose interests several countries had been devastated. So, he quit his job and decided to atone for his guilt henceforth by devoting himself uniquely to the saving of human lives."

"I see. Therefore, his roaming about with his cistern truck, to save men who were dying of thirst."

"Precisely. The only thirst he couldn't quench was his thirst for forgiveness."

"Now I can better understand his restlessness."

Meddur nodded in agreement.

"But how could he justify to himself years later that he had deliberately killed two dozen fighters? Had his anger made him do it? His thirst for revenge?"

"Not at all."

"What else, then?" I asked perplexed.

"You're not going to believe this. In that intervention he saw a kind of atonement for what he considered ever more as his cowardice, back then in Libya. And he didn't justify it through words but through a mathematical formula. After all, he was a thoroughly technically minded man. 'Twice negative results in positive,' that's what he said. That was mathematically irrefutable."

If the situation hadn't been so serious, I would have laughed out loud. It was the first time that I'd heard about a man who was trying to explain some existential problem by mathematics. Even scientific socialism hadn't gone so far. Bewildered and amused at the same time by what I had heard, I stood up from the ground and walked away from the acacia's shadow, accompanied by my own elongating shadow, to stretch my legs and smoke a cigarette.

Soon, Meddur appeared at my side.

Unexpectedly he continued with his philosophical deliberations. The desert, he said, was something like an expectation without expectation. It was teaching us to be open for everything, come what may. Without the void of the desert there was nothing, for only thanks to its void could we take enough distance from ourselves to come paradoxically very close to our souls.

"Only someone who loses himself can find himself again in the desert."

I was quite astonished at this contradiction, and I had no answer for it.

Meddur stooped down and drew some mysterious shapes in the sand.

"We humans are nothing but dust on the trail of the wind. We are the quicksand of the desert."

"But we do leave tracks," I threw in. "Perhaps not in the desert itself, but at its edge."

The Targi ruminated for a while before wiping out the shapes he had just drawn in the sand.

"Like Waterman you are so obsessed with the visible tracks that you can't see the invisible ones that constantly cross your life. I will tell you why the desert wipes out all traces: because it is a path and not a destination. It is a transition. When you stand still in the desert you die. Even so it is in life in general. Just look at the people who believe they have arrived at their destination and cling to what they have achieved. They are dead inside, because they congeal with fear of change, of movement, in short: of life itself."

I had to admit that there was some truth in this. Actually, this was true for all deserts, the horizontal ones as well as the vertical ones, the icy deserts and the hot ones, the ocean and even the sky. A boat that didn't move in the doldrums was lost. An airplane that didn't stay in motion had to fall from the sky. Life forbade immobility. Somewhere, there was always a safe harbor waiting, a landing strip, a distant shore. He was right: The desert connected life with itself. It wasn't an end in itself. It served life.

As if he had guessed my thoughts, Meddur mentioned a painting that Waterman had hung up in his tent. It showed nothing but a cloudless sky and a yellow-brown strip of earth beneath it.

"I never understood why he had chosen that painting for his home, since he had only needed to step in front of his tent to contemplate the real sky. In contrast to the painting, it was as changeable as life.

"'A painted sky is no sky,' I told Waterman.

"He answered that a painted sky was more than the sky.

"Uncomprehending, I shook my head, went to my tent where I built a small frame from four sticks. Then I went back to him and held the frame in front of his face by constantly changing its position.

"'Look, now you can see everything you want to see. If you hold the frame against the sky, you can only see the sky; against the earth, only the earth.' I was very proud of my demonstration.

"But he replied: 'Your frame doesn't show what one cannot see.'

"'What's that rubbish supposed to mean? Coming from a hopeless realist like you? Has the sun burnt your brain, or what? In your picture, too, you can only see the sky that the artist has painted there.'

"'Wrong! The picture comes alive through what it doesn't show. Think of the man who painted it. His physical shape is nothing. What he hides in himself is everything. And that's precisely what lives on in his picture after the artist has long disintegrated to dust.'

"'But the world is profound, too.'

"'Only because you look at it and recognize yourself in it.'"

The Targi took a break. He seemed to let these words run through his head again.

"I was puzzled because at that time I couldn't understand what he wanted to say, but I sensed there might be a hidden wisdom in his words. Also, perhaps, because those words came from him of all people, a man who usually thought in terms of facts and figures, of plan B's, of maps and scales. Was it possible that there lay hidden something more profound behind his jumble of figures and numbers? Perhaps what I couldn't or wouldn't see in his painting?"

Meddur pointed his finger at the stars in the sky.

"The enormous depth up there is nothing in itself," he said. "Today I can understand at last what Waterman was trying to tell me at that time."

"And what would that be?"

"In the desert night, Allah has only our eyes to see across to himself."

We returned to the acacia and sat down. For a while, only the shadowy silence wrapped us under the tree canopy. Then Meddur raised his voice again and conjured up images and emotions in me which sent tears to my eyes. Jonas Brunner had begun to develop a strange momentum in my imagination, and the *duar* of the Tuareg had finally pitched its tents in my heart.

"Although Waterman was desperately unhappy, he eventually recovered. His guilt feeling because of Kahina's death demanded of him to look after Lunja. He might have seen it as some weak form of atonement for the terrible loss the girl had endured. But when he approached her, she shied away and began to weep. Neither Waterman's good words nor his almost endless patience were any help. The girl blamed him for her mother's death, which increased his guilt feelings and confirmed his belief that he was carrying death in himself, and his fate condemned him to a life of loneliness, unless he wanted to plunge more people into misfortune.

"I tried to talk him out of it, but it was no use. Waterman walled his feelings in, to protect himself and others. As if to balance things, he worked harder and harder, drove his truck around the desert like a madman to distribute materials, to start new projects, and occasionally to add to the number of marks on his cabin door by saving lives.

"He probably took me along only because he owed me his life and seemed to have no deadly influence on me. Unfortunately, our talks gradually diminished to a few words and eventually petered out altogether, which was of no real importance because we had already become a well rehearsed team and each of us knew exactly what to do.

"One morning—we were lost in the east of nowhere—I saw him lie on his belly on the ground next to the truck and stare at a scorpion which was vigorously waving about its stingy tail in front of his nose. The strange spectacle went on for some time, while I remained completely motionless so as not to provoke a deadly sting by a careless movement. Eventually the scorpion lost interest and retreated.

"Waterman stood up and shook the sand from his clothes.

"'Fascinating,' he said, more to himself than to me, 'that life and death are so close together.'

"I was dumbfounded by such a defiance of death.

"When, driving on a bit later, I asked him what had motivated his brazen dance with death, he looked at me nonchalantly.

"'Nothing could have happened to me for I am as dangerous as the scorpion. I also carry the sting of death in me. Who knows when I'm going to direct it at myself?'

"Most reassuring, I thought, to be travelling through the murderous heat in the company of a suicide candidate.

"Lunja was taken care of by some relatives, as it is the custom in our clan. In the following years she became a beautiful young woman. Over time, her aversion towards Waterman abated, and eventually she even came along with us in the cistern truck."

After these words, Meddur spread out his prayer rug once more and performed his evening prayers, while I prepared a simple meal from canned food, which we later ate in silence.

Third Night

W HEN, AFTER OUR MEAL, Meddur had brewed a new pot of tea, he continued with his narrative.

"The craziest adventure with Waterman took place a few years later, when our *duar* had developed a great deal and other split off groups of nomads had joined us. Thereby the number of our people had grown considerably, and Waterman's water transports had to be undertaken at ever shorter intervals. Our lives depended completely on his cistern truck, for our well rendered far too small amounts of water to feed our population, which had grown to more than a hundred people. A gloomy sorrow darkened our spirit, for what would happen if Waterman had an accident or fell seriously ill? True, he had taught me a lot of things so that I might replace him in the worst case. But what if we both didn't return from one of our trips?

"When we discussed this danger with Waterman one day, he asked me unexpectedly what I thought of oil.

"'Why are you asking me this?'

"'Just answer.'

"'The oil is a curse for the *imohar*. Wherever they drill for oil the modern world invades the desert and the nomads are considered a nuisance. Overnight new settlements arise which endanger our way of life. And the wealth created by the black gold always flows into distant pockets anyway.'

"'Alright,' he said, and we didn't touch the subject again.

"Some months later an ATV with four people turned up. They were all dressed in overalls with a red and blue logo that read "Exxon." I hated that logo with the two x's in the middle resembling a barbed-wire fence. So, I kept my distance while Waterman approached the men to find out what they wanted.

"He seemed to know the leader of the group from his time as an engineer, for they embraced in a friendly way. The Exxon people produced some maps and appeared to negotiate in a lively way with him. Again and again, they looked up from their papers and pointed in this or that direction. I began to become wary, although I had great trust in Waterman.

"When the men had disappeared in their Jeep, I went to speak to my friend to learn what was going on.

"'Wait and see,' he answered mysteriously. 'Please fetch the diviner, old Ali.'

"'But . . . '

"'Get him and don't ask any questions.'

"Ali was our *marabut*, a master of the divining rod. Unfortunately, he hadn't found anything so far. Reminded of this, he always maintained that the treasures which he divined were really there, but they were too deep in the ground to be exploited.

"For this reason, he was often laughed at and not taken seriously by the other members of the clan. The only exception was Waterman, who often engaged in strange discussions with the old man.

"Ali and Waterman spent the days following the Exxon men's visit walking around behind the divining rod of the old man. I suspiciously observed their doings from the distance. In the end they stopped in a hollow between two hills situated towards the *Aïr*. Waterman dropped to one knee and looked around as if he wanted to memorize the spot. Then he wrote something in a little notebook.

"When I spoke to him about the strange procedure and wanted to know what the performance with the whimsical old man was all about, he only said it was about water against oil.

"Not finding this reassuring, I reminded him of our former talk about oil and its harmful side effects.

"But he only lifted his shoulders and gave me a resounding *inshallah*.

"Two days later, the Jeep with the oil guys reappeared. It was followed by trucks loaded with containers, pipes, tubes, and other parts of metal structures. Waterman fetched maps from his shed and joined them. After a short palaver he called Ali, who seemed to wait for this in the shade of a *seriba*. You should have seen the strange procession, Jean! At the head, Ali was hobbling behind his driftwood divining rod, and behind him followed an endless file of sweat-soaked Exxon overalls loaded with gauges, poles, and tripods. Bathed in sweat because of the burning heat, the white man with his technical world obediently followed the rod of wisdom of an African *Marabut*—science walking behind primitive belief, greed behind a mirage, and complexity behind simplicity. Despite my worries, I had to smile at this strange sight. The file of men—as was to be expected—walked to the spot that Ali had pointed out to Waterman with his divining rod on the previous day.

"On arriving there, Ali pointed at the ground and called in *Tamasheq*: 'Water!'

"'Indeed, oil!' translated Waterman into French and nodded in agreement.

"I stopped short. Which of those two was not quite there in his head?

"At once, the men unloaded the equipment they had brought along and began with their surveying work. Then they fetched the larger materials from their trucks and started to erect a derrick. Probably Waterman had used Ali only as a pretext for pointing out the position of oil reserves whose existence he had found out and marked on his maps long ago.

"I was speechless with disappointment. How could I have been so wrong about Waterman? This was Allah's punishment for entrusting the fate of the clan to an *ikufar*. Soon, there would be nothing left but to leave this place and look for another spring and new pastures elsewhere.

"Utterly cast down, I sat down on a nearby hill and watched what was going on.

"When the iron structure of the derrick was in place and heavy pipes had been mounted, the drilling work began. Soon, the black gold would shoot up and destroy our livelihood. I had to resist the impulse to run to Waterman's store shed, fetch a gun, and die for the *duar*. But that would only have meant death and ruin for the clan. So, I remained seated and surrendered to our seemingly inevitable fate.

"Suddenly there was a gurgling sound and what came out of the drilling hole was . . . water.

"The Exxon men looked at each other and seemed baffled.

"The head engineer's face flushed with anger under his contrasting white helmet as he turned to Waterman and looked at him questioningly.

"Grown curious, I approached the two men.

"Waterman shrugged his shoulders and tried to appear surprised.

"At this point the Exxon man lost his temper.

"'Are you fooling me?' he shouted. 'You dirty rat, you bloody cad, do you know how much a day like this costs us? And what about the transport of the equipment? Your stupid diviner is an absolute idiot. The sun must have fried your brain, you asshole!'

"Waterman did his best to calm him down.

"'Do you know, you stupid idiot, what we're going to do now? We're going to fill in that hole again. Your new friends shall see for themselves how they can get water.'

"At these words, Waterman's attitude changed completely. His features hardened. Taking hold of the far smaller engineer by his collar, he yelled at the fidgeting man's face. He told him he knew very well where to find oil, and as an experienced prospecting and extracting engineer, he wouldn't allow to be called names by a dirty little hole puncher like him. 'Do you really want oil? A sea of black slime? Then look hard, you dwarf, and learn something from me!'

"The baffled engineer, completely taken by surprise, stared with big eyes at the map which Waterman was spreading out before him.

"Jonas pointed at two or three positions on the map.

"'You're wasting your time if you scratch for oil here. I drew this map myself when I was tapping the desert for oil for Exxon. And as far as I know, nobody has ever exploited the locations marked on this map. So just calm down and listen: You leave this well open and in exchange you'll get this map.'

"'How can I be sure you're not fooling me again?'

"'This man here is going to come along with you in my truck. The truck represents my entire possessions. If you can't find oil at the first location marked on the map you may exchange my truck against a camel, on which my driver can ride back here. But if you find oil we are quits.'

"The engineer hesitated for a few moments, but since he had to make up for the costs of the expedition he finally agreed hesitantly and grumpily."

"And?"

"The Exxon men found an oilfield of huge proportions, over which the warring militias in the north are now fighting each other to the blood. On the other hand, the survival of our *duar* was secured for years with the new well thanks to Waterman's trick. When I returned from the trip north after ten days, I first went to see Waterman and told him about the successful development of the new oilfield. Before his happy grin could grow too broad, I came out with the accusing question that had been on my mind for several days.

"'Why didn't you tell me what you were planning?'

"'I told you exactly what I was planning: water against oil! But you seemed to have understood oil against water, my dear friend. The least one could expect from a storyteller is open ears to listen carefully.'

"Contrite, I swallowed down the reproach, for basically he was right.

"'Luckily there is only water and no oil near our *duar*,' I said to emphasize the fact that good fortune had also played a role in his plan.

"Puzzled, he looked at me.

"'Are you really so slow on the uptake? The deep strata of this ground are teeming with oil. The only thing Ali did with his rod was to find the one spot where there isn't any, but a lot of water instead.'

"My jaw dropped with astonishment, dear Jean, you can believe me. But really there was no reason for it, for I ought to have known that in life you can only ever find what you are looking for."

I doubtfully looked at Meddur. "And you want me to believe that?"

"You have to decide for yourself. For me, it is certainly the truth."

"What do you mean with this? Is it only the truth for you, or is it really the truth?"

"Who knows when truth turns into a story, and which of the two is more trustworthy?"

Irritated, I threw down my pen, because I had the unpleasant impression of having been fooled by an oriental fabulist.

Meddur smiled at my irritation and fumbled with the teapot.

To calm down, I walked away to smoke a cigarette in the shade of the stars.

When I returned to his side, Meddur asked me if I wanted to hear the end of his story, the *Kel Assuf* were getting a bit impatient.

"I am sorry," I said, "of course I'd like to hear the end of it, whether it is a true story or an invented truth."

At these words, the Targi laughed out loud with his croaking voice.

"Well then, now that the clan had enough water thanks to Waterman's trick, his activities were at first dedicated to the job of procuring materials for the enlarging of the well and the infrastructure of the *duar*. Somehow, I couldn't get rid of the impression that we were becoming settlers despite our self-image as herdsmen and hunters. He, on the other hand, as he had increasingly less to do in the *duar*, was gradually turning into a nomad who was migrating crisscross through the desert in his rolling whale. Most of the time I went along with him. Over time, he set his mind on improving my reading skills and my general knowledge. When it came to technical expertise, he gradually taught me everything that he knew himself.

"In one of his stores there were hundreds of dusty books piled up in a corner. He had probably taken them along when he left the destroyed oilfield in Libya after the departure of the *Al-Qaida* fighters. Waterman now made it a condition for me to take one of them with me to read whenever I wanted to come along with him.

"'Books and deserts have one thing in common, ' he said. 'When you look into them for answers, you will find questions.'

"In the beginning, my reading skills were rather poor, so that even a thin booklet like *Létranger* was enough to cross the entire desert. Gradually I got better, so that not even a fat volume of *À la recherche du temps perdu* was enough. The exercise brought both of us some advantages: My reading aloud shortened the journey for him, and through his corrections and explanations I learned a great deal about Western culture.

"Gradually, I began to measure the duration of a trip no longer in sunrises or like Waterman in kilometers, but in book pages. In a way, I leafed myself through the infinity of the desert. This nourished my mind and made distances shrink.

"I was only worried that the books, once put away, were like the dead. They lay there like princesses possessed by the *Kel Assuf* who were waiting for the kiss of a reader to be reawakened from death. My stories, on the other hand, lived and still live in me and with me, and they will live on in my descendants to whom I have related them countless times."

I interrupted Meddur with the remark that his story would one day also become a sleeping princess under my pen and therefore be immortal, because anyone could reawaken her to life at any time.

"Can such a thing really be called life?"

"No doubt. Just like all the books that you have read and that live on in you and won't die with you."

He seemed to be looking for an answer to my words but gave up.

As for myself, I understood at last why this nomad was so philosophical, so wise and so well read. The combination of the thousand year old orally transmitted wisdom of his people and the literary heritage of Western culture, which he had acquired through Waterman's mediation, made him a unique fountain of wisdom in the middle of this void.

After a long silence he continued with his story.

"Thanks to Waterman's inventiveness and managerial talent, there soon grew trees from the sand all over our settlement and beyond. The natural cycle of life was complete. Normally it is nature that completes the cycles broken up by humans. Here, for once, it was the other way round. A human being, by the power of his knowledge and his skills, managed to close a natural cycle that resisted the desert. He only achieved that by giving the water a higher priority than the oil. He had understood that oil is being taken away from the earth once and for all—according to a linear logic—but water flows back into the earth, which forms a natural cycle."

Meddur made a pause and sipped some tea before continuing with an emotional voice.

"One day, the inevitable happened. Waterman wanted to leave. He began to feel useless in our community. He needed new experiences, new adventures. His zest for action could no longer find enough satisfaction within the harmony of our *duar*. He had to leave to give his life a new purpose and to face other challenges. Our settled existence became a horror for the nomad in him. The roles were totally reversed: The European who was destined for a settled life was yearning for new horizons, while we nomads stayed tied down to a patch of earth. But that was what circumstances demanded. I tried to hold him back, invented new tasks for him, tried to make him believe how much we needed him. It was useless.

"When Waterman was caught up by unrest, nothing could hold him back."

"'You have water now and you know how to make the best of it. But as for me, I am needed where there's none. The Sahara is so large, and water is so rare. Yet my name is Waterman, and water must flow. And while the desert needs movement, the oasis needs tranquility. A tranquility which doesn't agree with me. I just cannot stay.'

"'And our friendship?'

"'I will carry it with me as long as it remains in your heart.'

"'These are words. Nothing can replace a person's presence.'

"'The traces that I'm leaving behind are indelible and attest to my friendship.'

"'I'm coming with you.'

"'No. You are the *Amghar* of the *duar*. Moreover, you carry my knowledge. The clan needs you.'

"Angry and frustrated as I was, I threw in his face that he was running away from his responsibility. But he only shrugged his shoulders and began with the preparations for his departure.

"When everything was ready, I stood there with drooping arms and tears in my eyes and felt like an orphan. But I also knew that nothing could oppose Allah's will. *Kismet* would have its way.

"Waterman went to see every villager to take his leave. When he came up to me, he was twitching around his mouth. He embraced me with unexpected passion, and then he was gone very quickly, so as not to betray his pain over this farewell.

"Soon afterwards, Jonas and his whale had disappeared behind the dunes. I had lost a friend, but I had gained a story."

"And what a story!" I commented with admiration. "You have never seen Waterman again?"

"Yes. One last time."

I looked at the shadowy spot where I imagined Meddur's eyes.

"Years went by," he took up the thread of his narrative. "My children had left our tent and given us seven grandchildren. The *duar* had grown into a considerable oasis. But often when life flourishes most powerfully death is nearest."

"The jihadists again?" I asked.

"No, even worse. A lot worse."

"I can't see what could be worse."

"The desert."

"The desert?"

"Yes. The death of our *duar* approached very slowly, silently. Soon, our oasis was no longer situated on the border between the steppe and the desert, but in the midst of sand dunes that surrounded it and grew ever higher. We could shovel and plant trees as much as we wanted, the circle was closing around us, and the *duar* was gradually covered in sand.

"The day wasn't far off when we would have to give up our useless fight and move to new waterholes and new pastures. The desert was advancing, and nothing could stop it.

"A few weeks before the cold season began—we had already started our preparations for our departure—Waterman appeared again. My heart began to beat hard when I saw him. But I knew that it was too late even for this rescuer from another world to do anything against the advancing desolation, because nobody can keep from the desert what it claims. We embraced. Despite the years, he seemed unchanged. There was still that lambent radiance in his eyes, that twitching of the corners of his mouth, and that inner unrest which only little signs rendered visible from the outside. Age didn't appear to have any influence on him. After he had greeted the other members of the clan, I offered him some tea.

"But he didn't respond to it and only looked round in astonishment."

"'You want to leave your *duar*?'

"'There is no alternative. You can see for yourself what the situation is like. Soon, our oasis will be one of the sunken settlements which the desert has incorporated.'

"'That must not happen!' he said with a coarse voice. 'It can be prevented.'

"There he was again, *ad-dalw*, the wonderful, daring man who believed he could extinguish the sun with a water hose. But this time, there were limits to his laudable intentions.

"I told him so.

"He replied with the story of the old donkey that was thrown down a shaft by a farmer to be buried alive. When the farmer began to shovel earth on top of it, the donkey shook it off and stamped on it with its hooves. Like this, it stood on what ought to have buried it, and gradually it reached the surface and stepped out of the shaft.

"'What we are dealing with here isn't earth but sand,' I sighed back and started to return to my jobs around the tent.

"But Waterman didn't appear to abandon his saving plan. For days on end, he walked through the *duar*, inspected the sand and the dunes, and scribbled all sorts of things in his notebook.

"Finally, he came back to me.

"'It is possible!' he said triumphantly.

"Then he showed me some sketches and plans of which I couldn't make any sense. The longer he explained his ideas, the more it seemed to me as if he wanted to lend some geometric forms to an absurd dream.

"'The enemy is not the sand but the wind. And wind can be channeled like water,' he said, his words tumbling over one another with enthusiasm. He seemed to have rediscovered the principle of Archimedes.

"Two slanted blocks of concrete should serve as foundations. On top of these there should be a stonewall that could be elevated as needed. Rocks were also part of the desert. One only had to defeat the desert with its own weapons. Static dunes, too, were solid inside and therefore resisted the constant changes of the sandy surface of the desert. I should stop the preparations for our departure. He would start work immediately.

"And he grabbed me by my shoulders, shaking them as if he wanted to bring down some dates from my turban.

"'The *duar* is as good as saved! Believe me.'

"Well, my credence remained somewhat limited.

"'That won't hold for long,' I replied in a mild voice. 'The Sahara is the largest hourglass in the world. It never stops because there will always be sand and always more sand. Only that the sand trickles in all directions and not from top to bottom.'

"'But sand can be rerouted like water.'

"'You give in to illusions. Any bulwarks against the desert are ruins even before they are built. For a time, they offer some protection, but then they are swallowed up by the sand. Nothing built with sand or stones can be stronger than the desert. Even man is sand and returns to sand.'

"Waterman's face went pale when he realized the unconditional state of my refusal. I know, he was a white man. But most of the time he was red in his face. Now he really turned white or pale or even grey, I don't know. Something like that. It was a hue that came from inside, not from outside and not from his skin either.

"When I turned my back on him and devoted myself to the dismantling of the tent again, he remained standing there with drooping arms. A salt pillar in a fossilized sea.

"A few days later, our caravan set off.

"Jonas Brunner walked to his vehicle with tired steps. Soon he disappeared with his water carrying whale in a northern direction, while we headed west on the humps of our camels. Each to his destiny, each on his journey, *inshallah.*"

Meddur meditated for a while before adding a last comment.

"I had withheld from Waterman that there had been another reason for our departure. Being a driven type, paradoxically, he wouldn't have understood. We had been overtaken by the drive of the nomads. The yearning for movement. We were attracted by different grounds, palm trees and springs in the everlasting and yet always changeable Sahara. We followed the call of the unwritten laws of the desert, the call of the migrating herds and of the seasons. We followed the rain, which eluded us most of the time.

"The *imohar* who doesn't want to get lost in his inner desert has to confront the outer desert. Eye to eye. Sand grain to sand grain. For the desert is a home without a house, a domicile without a shelter, a foothold without land. Though unrooted, the *imohar* is rooted in it, do you understand? He only knows the occupation— without possession—of an unlimited border area.

"The true home of the Tuareg is the journey, and our house is the camel. We are one with the animal that carries us. In union with it, we become a *mehari*. And the *mehari* is the road, is the caravan, is life on the whole."

At this point, Meddur's voice failed. He seemed to be overcome by emotions.

"A few days ago, my own camel died after forty years of companionship. Now it is waiting for me somewhere up there."

So, finally, I got to know why the Targi was waiting for death under his lonely acacia. He was too old to join a union with a new animal, but he was not able to survive in the desert without a camel.

Not knowing what to say, I let Meddur decide whether he wanted to resume the thread of his narrative or not.

He didn't utter another word for quite some time. Then he stood up to urinate under the glow of the stars.

When he returned—it was long after midnight, and my throat felt strangely parched with all that tea I'd had—he wrapped himself up in his blanket and seemed to want to go to sleep.

The moment had come to say goodbye. If I made a start right now, I could cover a good distance before daybreak. I didn't feel tired, anyway.

"That was certainly a beautiful story," I said. "But seriously, Meddur, is it really true?"

"It is so true that an invented story couldn't be any truer," he replied.

Again, I felt terribly disillusioned. So, it was just another story among the thousands which regularly light up around campfires to scare off the spirits of the night. Meddur seemed to feel my disappointment.

"Do I still know myself what is true or not of my story? Maybe I have really invented it. Maybe I have just added all sorts of things to a core which was true. Maybe it has really happened like that. My old head cannot really tell the difference. Lately, it seems to me as if everything I have ever thought might be flowing together to form some higher version of reality."

"But . . . "

"Let's put it this way, my dear Jean: As long as you believe in the possibility of my oasis, my story is true."

A bit frustrated I stood up, shook the sand off my clothes and began to collect my belongings.

"You want to leave already?"

"I have to."

"A pity. You are missing the most important part."

"What do you mean?"

"My story isn't finished yet."

It was like being struck by lightning.

"Not finished yet?"

"The great finale is still missing."

"So, you met Waterman once more?"

"In some way."

"What's that supposed to mean?"

"If you want to know you'll have to sit down again."

I didn't know what to do. Was the old guy making fun of me? Did he only want to hold me back to postpone his death a little? Or . . . ? My curiosity won and I sat down again, while Meddur fumbled with his teapot and the gas cooker again.

When we had sipped the first cup to the dregs and I was furious with hidden impatience again, he continued with his story, which in fact should have been finished.

"For years and years, we wandered about the desert and only just survived on the crest of deprivation by constant movement. The Scirocco and the Samum drove us ahead of them like tumbling bushes. We could count the numbers of the few raindrops which fell on us. But we pushed on, as free people. And every new day that Allah—*La hauwla wa la Quwwata illa billah*—sent us from heaven filled us with awe. We were poor in terms of sterile money, but the fertility of our women and camels made us rich. We hardly had enough to eat, but the little we had was a lot, for it did not narrow us down.

"One day in spring, in the southwest of the *Aïr*, on the edge of the great void, our caravan suddenly lost its way. *L'agedelsit sem-midet*, the space of the fresh morning, came to its end when we lost control and began to drift among the dunes."

"How was that possible?"

"The camels. They suddenly refused to obey us. Try as we might to force them back, they stubbornly walked in a certain direction which they had probably been talked into by Allah."

"And?"

"I got out my binoculars and searched the glimmering emptiness before us. There was nothing. Nothing but sky and sand. But the camels accelerated their pace as if they had smelt grass or water. The situation was getting a bit weird. But we consoled ourselves with the thought that our camels were as reliable as the will of Allah, and we let go of the reins.

"When we had come on top of a tall dune, we nearly fell down the other side which was almost a vertical drop. In front of us there stretched an empty space that made even the void of the desert look like a field of abundance. Looking down, we saw that there were some palm trees and acacias growing at the bottom of a tub like cleft.

"It hit me like lightning!

"This was the work of Waterman, his last stand against the desert! Without realizing, we had returned to his oasis. How was it possible that I hadn't guessed it when our camels had gone their own way? Probably because I had mentally buried our former *duar* under the sand beneath which I thought it might lay.

"But the fact was that Jonas Waterman had split the desert! The dunes followed the wind channels that he had planned for them and bypassed the *duar*. The sand submitted to Waterman's will, and the winds blew as he had directed them. His construction resembled a huge ship in the surf. Pointed at the prow and broad at the stern, it let the storms of life and even the passage of time flow past it imperturbably. Later I found that—immobile and firmly anchored as it was—it appeared to be traveling through the sand in times of strong winds, although it was the sand which was moving past it."

I shook my head in doubt. The description reminded me too much of the Bible, which must have been part of Meddur's standard reading during his trips in the truck: "When Waterman lifted his pole above the desert the Lord made it recede by a strong eastern wind through the whole night, and revealed a well and the dunes separated," I parodied the Bible in my mind.

After Meddur had prepared and poured the second round of tea he continued.

"Like the winds, we circumnavigated the site and approached the valley from the other side, where the margins were deeper and allowed an easier access. You should have seen that, my dear Jean. We found ourselves surrounded by a palm grove which could have measured up to the one of Bilma. All around us blooming laurel bushes, tamarisks, and acacias. Pomegranates and fig trees along our path. Next to these there grew wheat, barley, millet, and vegetables. Then we came to a pasture where goats and camels were grazing. I felt a pang in my heart: the oasis was occupied already! Our former *duar* had become the home of another tribe! But the person who finally approached us was a single man dressed in oriental clothing. When I dismounted from my camel and walked up to him, I had the greatest surprise of my life. I was facing Waterman, only much younger and stronger than I remembered. It was as if he had fallen into a Fountain of Youth.

"Unbelieving, I greeted the rejuvenated image of my lost friend.

"'Assalamu Alaykum.'

"'Assalam.'

"'Please excuse my consternation, stranger, it is only . . . your face . . . you remind me of an old friend.'

"'So, you are Meddur', he replied to my amazement. 'I have been waiting for you a long time.'

"'You know who I am?'

"'Jonas Brunner was my father.'

"'Was? He is no longer among the living souls?'

"'I'm afraid not.'

"'But how . . . ?'

"'Around the neck of his dead body there was a sort of plastic envelope with two letters inside. One of them was addressed to me, the other one to you. But pardon me, I am neglecting my duties of hospitality. We will look at the letters later. The heat is heavy already, and you must be exhausted from your journey. Just settle in, for this place is yours. As its guardian I am commissioned by my father to hand it over to you.'

"That Jonas Brunner, I thought, that lovely old fox! He had managed even beyond death to implement the craziest plan B the earth had ever seen. And this time I definitely couldn't contradict him."

Meddur fell silent. He was obviously indulging himself in pleasantly painful memories.

"The desert surrounds our secrets with an even greater secret," he finally said and yieldingly sighed before he continued.

"When my people had unloaded the camels and lain down in the shade of the palm- trees and bushes to take a nap and wait for the end of the hottest time of the day, I joined Brunner junior, who was sitting on a pillow in the shade of a fig-tree, preparing tea. When he saw me, he invited me to sit down on a free pillow opposite. Silently I watched him strew the tea leaves in the pot with confident and elegant movements. He added sugar and finally brought the beverage to bubble with swaying up and down movements like an old Bedouin. The tea was delicious.

"'My name is Peter', he introduced himself.

"'Delighted. You already know mine.'

"He nodded.

"'You probably ask yourself how it can be that I have been waiting for you for quite some time.'

"'You can certainly say that,' I said and looked at him in expectation.

"'Well, before I hand you my father's letter, I must tell you the story which led to its being written.

"'As you may know, my parents got divorced when I was eight years old. Their separation didn't happen the same way as in most other cases, in which the parents fight over custody and alimony and the father is finally granted the right to spend every other weekend with his child. My father had just disappeared from one day to the next. There was no fight, no legal wrangling, no fat lawyers' fees. My father saw his only victory over my mother in his escape, so he just left. That was worse than if they'd had a proper fight. Because like that I would at least have had the impression that I mattered to them. But like that? My father didn't seem to want me, and my mother seemed to have to want me. Somehow, I felt orphaned. Even worse: betrayed of the love that I considered was due to me. As time went by, my absent father began to haunt me. It may seem absurd to feel obsessed with an absence. And yet it was like that. I began to hate my father because I missed him. And because my hatred led to nothing, I began to hate myself. My mother couldn't do anything about it. I was listless and apathetic, I kept company with broken down types and finally fell victim to drugs. My relationship with my mother was in a shambles. I isolated myself. If I couldn't have a father, I didn't want a mother either. We lived like strangers in the same house, for she didn't manage to throw me out.'

"'Then, one day, there was a letter from my father in our mailbox, in which he asked me to find an oasis in the loneliness of a distant desert region, to look after it and finally to hand it over to some nomad called Meddur, who would appear with his tribe one day in the future. Suddenly, everything was different. Henceforth I had a mission, an objective. I had a father who was counting on me even beyond death.

"'First, I had to get off the drugs. That didn't just happen by itself, you can believe me. I suffered like a dog. Then I had to get the money for the journey. I worked hard in menial jobs on building sites and helped with the garbage collection, until I had the required sum. I couldn't expect anything from my mother, since she considered my father's letter a mad fantasy. But she didn't try to hold me back either. In principle it was okay for her if I left the apartment. I can't really blame her, given my earlier behavior.

"'When, after my crossing from Europe to Africa, I saw the desert for the first time, I knew that I couldn't venture into it without preparation if I didn't want to risk my life. It was breathtakingly dangerous. Deadly beautiful. So, I joined a camel driver and learned on various expeditions to submit to the unwritten laws of the desert. In the process, I began to understand what had attracted my father to this place. I also felt the same irresistible appeal of the endless space, the challenge of the untamable, the irresistible call of the desert. I became its lover, but at first, I rather felt like a male mantis before the mating act. In due course, this obsessive image disappeared. I began to love the dangers of the desert, because they sharpened my senses and required my undivided attention. I learned to live an intensive and unconditional life and to master the risks without agitation. At last, I felt ready and set out on my quest for that impossible spot in the middle of nowhere which was marked with a little cross on a map. Again and again, I was overcome by doubts. Perhaps the place I was looking for would turn out to be a *fata morgana*, perhaps I was just imagining something, and my father had just played a practical joke on me. All the same, I continued my search. I read and reread the letter many times, studied the carefully noted degrees of latitude and longitude, which I soon knew by heart, and followed the plan, unflustered. Finally, I was successful. On finding my destination I also found myself."

Meddur interrupted his narrative. I heard a rustling noise when he pulled a letter from his coat, offered it to me and said: "When Peter had completed his story, he got this envelope from his *gandura* and gave it to me."

I accepted the envelope, pulled out the sheet of paper and read.

My dear Meddur,

If these lines ever reach you, I'll have disappeared into those glittering pastures of your starry sky. But before I leave the world, I will defeat death by a plan B which will reach far beyond it. My plan B is the written word, which you distrust so much.

Should someone ever present these lines to you, you will hear my voice from the hereafter, which means that I'll have won a last victory over fate.

You will hardly believe it, dear Meddur, but I am stuck in a wadi that's gone wild. All around me, a torrential flash flood is raging which was caused by the first autumn storms on the Atlas. Rocks and sludge keep me captive in my truck. The water in the cabin is rising inexorably and already reaches up to my knees.

So much water! So little use for it!

Time has come to take farewell. I am doing this by solving a last riddle which I gave you a long time ago.

Do you remember me telling you that it would be life and not death which would eventually defeat me? Well, it's happening at this very moment.

I need not tell you, the imohar, that water means life in the desert. And it is precisely this water which is now putting a dignified end to my life. Desert, heat, sandstorms and thirst couldn't thwart my plan B's. Now I will—as crazy as it may sound—drown in the desert.

And yet, this grotesque departure makes sense!

Remember one thing, dear Meddur: We humans are always defeated by what we value the highest. I was a water carrier, and it is only right that Jonas Brunner, nicknamed Waterman, should shortly drown in his rolling whale.

Farewell, my friend, and always keep my remembrance in your heart, as I have cherished yours ever since our paths separated. One day, you will hit upon a trace that I have left for you and that I bestow upon you as a present in gratitude.

Allah's plan B is death. Mine is life.

fi amanillah, farewell,

ad-dalw.

The message of this letter was so unbelievable that I first thought Meddur had written it himself. But the handwriting! The style. And it often happened indeed, when winter broke earlier than expected, that people in a *wadi* were taken by surprise by a torrential flush flood and lost their lives.

I inserted the letter back into the envelope, with the intention to hand it back to Meddur.

"Keep it. Where I am going, letters are of no use. With it, you have proof of the fact that Waterman really existed."

Then, after three days and nights in my company, the Targi began to prepare the third pot of tea. It was probably the last one he would enjoy. To the dregs, like his life.

"What happened then with your tribe? And with Peter?" I asked.

"The tribe settled in the oasis. Apart from agriculture, we relied on a bit of hunting and trade. Thanks to Waterman's inventiveness we did well. For many years, I transmitted my knowledge to the younger people. When my wife died, I stepped down as *Amghar* and devoted myself to prayer and meditation. Now that even my camel has left me, nothing holds me back in this world."

"And Peter?"

"He stayed with us and married Lunja, with whom he had five children. Three boys and two girls. You can believe me, those two represented a perfect balance between hot and cold, as it exists between rider and camel. He fair haired like straw, with deep blue eyes, she brown haired with black pupils. That is how different the faces of the desert can be, just to belie the cliché. You should have seen the wedding. Just imagine: for the first time in the history of our people the dowry was a whole oasis. Five goats and ten sheep were slaughtered. Festivities lasted for over a week. And Peter showed a remarkable mastery in the *ahal*—the ritual courting. With him we were given back a part of *ad-dalw*. The part that needs the earth to grow. Sometimes it happens that a restless man's son can grow roots. It's all about *Kismet*."

Later, when everything had been said that needed to be said, Meddur asked a last but strange question: "I know that our oral tradition is doomed, for where there are no ears anymore, there won't be any mouths either. But are you sure that what you are recording and writing down will last into the future?"

"Of course. Writing sticks. Even today, we can read texts that were written down over two thousand years ago. Isn't that the case with your writing too, the *tifinagh*?"

"What's the use of it when no one can or wants to read the writing anymore?"

"How do you mean that?"

"Your written tradition might face the same doom as our oral one. Where the eye is blinding itself, the head will eventually get lost, too. And once the head is gone, nobody will resurrect the writing."

Long after switching off my recording device, I had to think of these words. While I was busy turning around arguments and counterarguments in my head, my eyelids became heavy, and I fell asleep.

The Morning After

W HEN I WOKE UP the next morning, the Targi was gone. He
had left the place during the night and had joined his last
breath to the desert wind.

I imagined how it must have been: He had got up very quietly
and had carefully placed a carved talisman in the shape of a cross
on the rug on which he had slept. Then he had followed the shadows of the *Kel Assuf* as they moved out to the desert. He had looked
up to the sky, so as to go through all the star constellations above
his head for the last time: the back of the camel mare, *amanar*,
the caravan leader, the camel stallion and the herd of Aldebaran,
which grazes the glittering grasses of the night.

Then he'd walked in the direction of Mecca and *l'eheren en
tufat*, the first shimmer of the new day. Soon, daylight had broken.
And suddenly there had been only light, and he had resolved in it.

I looked up to the waning stars in the sky and asked myself
in which of the heavenly camel pastures he could have found his
home.

As I was collecting my belongings it seemed to me as if I was
waking from a dream. If there hadn't been Meddur's rug, his teapot,
the talisman, and the letter, I would have doubted my own senses.
I thoughtfully sat behind my Land Rover's steering wheel and for
the last time looked at the acacia, whose branches had shielded our
human palaver for three days and three nights. Before turning the
ignition key, I panicked for a split second, fearing the car might not

start. But then I heard the humming of the engine and leaned back with a sense of relief.

There isn't anyone more reliable than a mechanic who has spent his whole life on the back of a camel.

Epilogue

W HEN, SEVERAL DAYS LATER, I played my recordings to myself in Agadez, the recorder went on while I was thinking of what I had heard. Suddenly there was a crackling noise and then Meddur's voice came on again for the last time.

"You have fallen asleep, my friend", the familiar voice said. "When you wake up, I will have become a shadow among shadows. But even the shadows of the *imohar* are given a voice. If you should hear this, I have pressed the right button on your machine.

"There is one thing I have to say before I leave, even though it might disappoint you. Please give up your crazy project! It is too late to reintroduce nomadic life in the desert. The inner desert has overcome the outer desert for a long time. And you can't plan the Sahara anyway. It is its own plan.

"Our *duar* is doomed, too. Not because it is threatened by holy warriors and shifting sand dunes, but because the temptations of the so called civilized world attract our young people to the cities. Their interest in our life of freedom in the desert is dwindling. They are dreaming of solid walls and a settled life in closed rooms.

"Soon, only old people will remain in the oasis, and no one will listen to their stories and spread them anymore.

"Yes, we used to be dreaded warriors, but that was a long time ago. Just imagine, our last raid was in 1934. Since then, things have been going down with us, because the world of the gardens have gradually overgrown the world of the raids. When money began to replace our traditional bartering, contact with the settlers became inevitable. And as we had to leave the border area of the desert because of the drought, at the same time the pressure of the population in the south increased. Agriculture was pushing north. Thus, we first became semi nomads who rented out their dwellings, then impoverished settled farmers who tried to eke out a living on the edge of society. Also, feudalism was abolished in the new independent states. Consequently, our *iklan* became settled and well to do, while we were, and have been to this day, busy with the administration of our ever dwindling resources. It has always been a rule that the rich man has his say. For decades, therefore, the settled people have been making the laws. They cut off old trade routes, issue bans and prohibitions for violations of the law, separate ethnic groups, and isolate tribes, while we are unable to stand against those developments. Therefore, the settlers don't feel constrained to abide by their own laws, not even the contractually agreed northern limitations for their crops of millet and peanuts.

"We, the Tuareg, are too individualistic to be interested in politics and not educated enough for big words and great ideas. The train of modernity has left without us. What remains for us but to settle on a poor strip of pasture and to come to an arrangement with the cattle owners of the south, which amounts to a tightrope walk of existence. Many of us hang out in reservations, living from hand to mouth, or take on small jobs as occasional workers in the mining and oil industries. Thus, our culture is gradually dying out.

"We have become like perishable goods the morning after market day.

"Our world is vanishing.

"But the desert, my dear Jean, the desert lives on. And where there is a desert there is hope, for what the desert gives nourishes without saturating and waters without quenching our thirst.

> *The human heart is made of sand,*
> *That's pushed around by stormy blows,*
> *The grains drift through the endless land,*
> *Till they become a sandy rose."*

After repeated perusal of the lyrical conclusion in the Berber language, which was very difficult to understand for me, I put the tape recorder away in disappointment. How was it possible for any hope to exist after such an assessment of the situation? And worse, I felt so stupid with my revival project for nomadic culture.

During the following years, I restlessly drove crisscross through the *Ténéré* in search of Meddur's *duar*. It had to exist somewhere, that wonderful oasis that withstood the desert although it had been made by man. Somewhere in the middle of nowhere, tall palm trees were swaying their heads in the fire and cooling their feet in the water. Hidden behind high dunes, children were playing hopscotch with the shades, children with a dark skin and eyes so blue that they seemed to look at you like two deep lakes. Somewhere in the big void, amidst the profusion of hallucinations, there was a dream which had become reality.

But its access was denied to me like the Promised Land was denied to Moses.

All the same, that oasis is still alive in my soul.

It will continue to live on in me as long as I keep looking for it. And as long as I keep looking for it, I will stay alive.

Should I find the oasis one day, I would lose the desert. And by losing the desert I would lose my soul.

Written in Corsica and finished in Tschärmilonga
during the winter of 2019–2020